"HOUSTON, WE'VE GOT A BOGIE!"

"Callisto Explorer, repeat please."

"We've got a bogie. Closing on the orbit of Jupiter. Estimated speed one hundred thousand miles per second. Mass estimated at three-zero-zero-zero tons. Houston, we are tracking. Bogie on collision course with planetary mass. This thing is really something! Put this baby on the ground and you could lay four football fields inside her length."

"Callisto Explorer, where is your bogie now?"

"She's going to pass behind the planet relative to us in approximately five minutes, Houston. Hold it. There was some sort of activity aboard the bogie. A glow. Houston, she slowed faster than is possible. We're losing her now, Houston . . ."

SIGNET Science Fiction You'll Enjoy

PRESSURE MAN

by
Zach Hughes

A SIGNET BOOK
NEW AMERICAN LIBRARY
TIMES MIRROR

PUBLISHER'S NOTE

This novel is a work of fiction. Names, characters, places, and incidents are either the product of the author's imagination or are used fictitiously, and any resemblance to actual persons, living or dead, events, or locales is entirely coincidental.

COPYRIGHT © 1980 BY HUGH ZACHARY

SIGNET, SIGNET CLASSICS, MENTOR, PLUME, MERIDIAN AND NAL BOOKS *are published by The New American Library, Inc., 1633 Broadway, New York, New York 10019*

FIRST PRINTING, NOVEMBER, 1980

1 2 3 4 5 6 7 8 9

PRINTED IN THE UNITED STATES OF AMERICA

o 1 o

If he had been asked to rely on public transport he would have refused to make the trip. He hated the crowded, clanking, sooty, coal-burning multicarriers with their surly Civil Service attendants. He hated surface travel in general, finding the contrast between the clean, empty reaches of space and the decaying planet to be almost nauseous.

He did not, as did many spacers, hold a belligerent contempt for old Earth. She was, after all, the source, the only source of many things, the mother of all, home. She reeked and rotted and continued to condone the overproduction of Goethe's man, so admirable in the individual, so deplorable in his masses. He did not feel contempt for Earth herself, only her people. He showed his impatience by growling obscenities as he was forced to the blown dunes at the side of the two remaining lanes of what once had been a four-lane superhighway to allow passage of a big drone cargo carrier.

He mopped perspiration from his forehead as he waited for the drone to clear, then steered the antique auto back onto the potholed road. The auto's air-conditioning unit had been removed, not too neatly, leaving a gaping hole in the dash. Most of the lining had been torn from the vehicle's roof, leaving only a thin

1

layer of metal between him and the desert sun. The engine, modified to burn methane, stank, coughed, wheezed, and strained as he tried to regain speed. The poorly engineered tank on the back of the car was definitely not aerodynamic. The dry cross wind made handling a nightmare when, by coaxing and cursing and pushing to the limit, he once again attained fifty miles per hour.

When he reached the low mountains the auto inched its way upgrade and bucketed downgrade with the heavy tank trying to fishtail. He growled grand and manly profanities at the car, the hot sands, the barren rocks, the decaying road. He saved a few choice words for the Department of Space Exploration and all those involved in sending him into the heat of the desert in a ground car which should have been scrapped a decade ago.

A drone, the second he'd met since leaving the city which sprawled over every available inch of land from the desert to the sea, screamed a warning siren at him. He found a lay-by, just in time, and the drone rumbled by, antennae wriggling like the feelers of a giant insect. He could see the crest of the low range of hills. He eased upward, the radiator on the verge of boiling. Then it was downhill, the engine cooled, and the speed created an illusion of coolness as wind whipped his hair into his face.

Heat waves shimmered over the flat lands. He met an auto, a relatively new model, probably one of the last production run, making it less than ten years old. It displayed a government seal on hood and doors. The driver was the first human he'd seen since leaving the city. He felt a childish desire to wave.

With easier driving, he allowed his mind to wander from the chore of keeping the shock-worn vehicle on the road and speculated about the reason for his being ordered to DOSEWEX, Department of Space Exploration West. His conclusion was that he had no idea. He was an engineer. He was a spacer. It was a good bet that he was not being called into the desert to be reprimanded. His record, for the past two years at least, was clean. He hadn't slugged a superior officer since then, and he had served his restriction time for that one. He'd spent one full year with all the little extras forbidden, one year during which his special rations had been divided among the other crew members, one full year without ground leave, not even on Moon Base. Then, just when he thought he was set for a holiday, and was making good progress with that long-legged communications officer in L.A. Operations, he got orders to report, in all haste, to DOSEWEX, way to hell and gone in the New Mexico desert.

The sun was low behind him when he reached the outer perimeter of the base. He got out of the car, stretched, knocked dust off his uniform, and allowed a detection machine to snoop him. He stood aside as the vehicle was searched and snooped. It was standard operating procedure. You couldn't control every yoyo in a population of three hundred million potential nuts, but you could limit their access to prime areas.

When he was passed through the perimeter guard post, he saw only more barren country ahead, but he was near enough to be able to look forward to a drink, a bath, a meal, in that order. A robot flagman slowed him. He steered the auto around a line of construction machines moving slowly in his own direction. Halfway past the group of large machines the flagman signaled him to pull in and he found himself directly behind a huge transport mounting a hefty crane. The crane transport seemed to be the control vehicle for the entire convoy of diggers and earthmovers. It was manned. He blew his horn, asking for a little cooperation in being allowed to pass. The base was near. He could see, off to his right, the profile of a low building. He inched forward to be in position to use the auto's feeble acceleration when he was given the go-ahead to pass, bringing the hood of his vehicle under the overhanging boom of the crane.

The operator of the transport seemed to be deaf. He leaned out the window and yelled, blowing his horn. He checked the shoulder, to see if he could pull off and pass on the right. He caught a flash of motion out of the corner of his eye.

On a scale of ten his reaction time was a ten plus. It was one of his best-known abilities, his quickness. More than once lightning reflexes had served him well, and they served him again as he slammed on the brakes, rocking the old vehicle on its worn shocks. At the same time, foot still pressed on the brake, he threw himself to his right and hit the floorboard just as the falling boom of the crane crushed the flimsy roof. The auto was being dragged forward as the crane transport continued to move. There was a grinding sound as metal folded and tore. Smoke came from the locked tires of the auto. It went on for perhaps thirty seconds before the boom pulled off the crushed roof to bend the hood. The cooling fan clanked against metal. The engine sputtered and died. The car was motionless.

He sighed and relaxed. Then he was jolted as the drone earthmover behind him rammed the car, continued pushing until the car slewed sideways to the blade of the earthmover. He could hear the car falling to pieces. There was a scrape of protesting metal and another jolt as the forward motion stopped, the auto rammed up under the boom against the rear of the crane transport, crushed, held tightly.

Once again he relaxed. He was alive. He was lying in a constricted space, the roof of the car pushed down to the seat bottom, the sides pushed in toward him. He smelled escaping methane and felt a tightening of every muscle in his body, but when seconds passed without an explosion, he tried to peek through a tiny slit which had once been a window. He heard movement outside. He had glass shards on his face and he was afraid to blink his eyes lest he cause glass splinters to fall from his hair and eyebrows into them.

"Are you all right?" a voice asked, from outside the crushed vehicle.

"The gas is leaking," he yelled. "Get some foam on this crate."

Footsteps moved away, not fast. He had a piece of jagged metal punching into his back. He tried a move to ease it. He was not badly hurt. He could move legs, arms, his back, his neck. Part of the seat back was on top of him. He pushed on it until he could see out of the slit of crushed window. He heard footsteps coming back.

"Get some foam on this wreck before it blows," he yelled.

He could see legs in blue work pants and service shoes. The man was standing quite near.

"Yeah, just take it easy," the voice said.

He heard a clank, a loud hiss. He froze. Gas was now escaping rapidly from the tank at the rear. And there were more sounds. He froze, not believing it. A small pop. The workman had just activated a self-igniting cutting torch.

"Turn that thing off, you dumb bastard," he screamed. "The gas is leaking."

"Yeah," the workman said.

The blue-clad legs moved. He saw the flame at the tip of the cutting torch and knew what was going to happen. He braced the back of his neck against the caved-in roof of the auto and pushed, momentarily panicked. He heard the methane ignite, whooshing into flame. He felt the heat immediately, and the rank odor of combustion was in his nostrils. Like millions, billions before him, he was thinking, "No, not me. Not now. Not yet."

Burning paint filled the crushed cab with smoke. The heat was a blast furnace. Evil black tendrils of heavy smoke snaked up into the small area in which he was trapped. A sheet of flame sprang up outside the slit of the window, cutting off his view of the world.

His mind was surprisingly clear. In a few seconds the entire tank of gas would go. At least it would be quick, one massive blow as the explosion fireballed up. At least it would be quick.

o 2 o

J.J. Barnes was no angel. He never had been and, unless he did a lot of changing, he never would be. Precise, calm, methodical, overbearing, yes. Angelic, no. Tall, graying at the temples, eyes cold gray behind functional rimless glasses, he towered over the world, his face just as remembered, smooth-shaven, masculine, almost handsome. But he was not an angel.

All this was evident in a slow swim upward into awareness. The world was J.J.'s face, and it was a burning world, and there was a stench of burning garbage gas.

His feet hurt. He lifted his head and looked down his body. His feet were bandaged.

"It isn't too bad," J.J. said. "It's painful, I know, but the damage is minor. That sore spot you feel on your ass is the only place they had to take skin for grafting."

He turned his head and saw a hospital table with water pitcher, pill tray, glass, and a small vase of roses.

"Are you with me, Flash?" J.J. asked.

The use of his old nickname helped him bring his eyes into full focus. "I think so," he said.

"That bastard had passed a double screening," J.J. said. "Are you ready to hear about it, or do you want to let your head clear a bit more?"

"Water," he said.

7

"Sure." J.J. poured and he took the glass, almost letting it slide through his fingers.

"Thanks," he said. He felt a twinge of soreness on his left buttock. The world tilted a little, then stabilized. He drank, and J.J. took the glass. "OK," he said.

"Flash, we can't keep all of them out. No matter how we try we can't screen all of them out. There are too many of them. They've been infiltrating too long, and some of them are damned smart."

"Why me?" he asked.

"Probably because you had a DOSE decal on your auto," J.J. said. "Working for DOSE is reason enough."

He was looking at his feet. They were bandaged from the calves downward. He wiggled a toe and it moved and there was only a small pain. He could feel the motion, but he couldn't see it through the bandages.

"They've got the pain senders blocked off," J.J. said.

"Yeah. I've been burned before."

"They're not as bad as you might think. One spot on the right instep had to have a graft. With these new methods you'll be on your feet in no time."

"I know about burns," he said. "What I don't know is why the administrator of DOSEWEX is taking time to hold my hand personally. And I don't quite buy your reasoning why some yoyo tried to kill me. I can't quite see it as an accidental selection, based on my being in a DOSE vehicle. And while I'm wondering, I wonder why said administrator of DOSEWEX pulled me away from my first ground leave in two years to come out into the desert to be almost burned to death."

J.J. chuckled.

"Dammit, J.J.," he said. "I want to know what's going on."

"My old ball-carrying buddy," J.J. said, shaking his head with an uncharacteristic expression of kindliness on his face. "Just take it easy. Eat, drink, and rest. You'll be walking in a couple of days."

He turned his head to try to see the sore spot on his rump. It, too, was bandaged. "When you went back to pass, I should have let those cadets cream you," he said.

"If you had, who would have spread your fame as the man who pulled the Army game out of the fire, excuse the reference, in oh-6? Now you take a nap like a good little aging running back and I'll see you in two days."

"J.J., you didn't send for me just to pay me compliments," Dom said. "What's going on?"

J.J. put his hands behind his ears and looked around the room. Dom got the message. The hospital room had not been swept. The walls could have ears.

"There'll be a couple of base investigators in here shortly," J.J. said. "Just tell them the truth about what happened. Tell them you were coming to DOSEWEX on the invitation of your old friend, the administrator, to talk over old times and have a drink or two. Tell them you have no idea why you were singled out as a target for terrorists."

"Just the truth," Dom said.

"When you're up and around I'm sure you'll enjoy our friendly little visit."

Dom sighed wearily. "I was invited by my old classmate, who kissed ass and got promotions. I have no idea why I was attacked. That last, at least, is the truth."

J.J.'s look was serious. "Just cool it, Dom."

Two uniformed security men stood beside his bed and asked the same questions repeatedly, getting the same answers repeatedly. Just the facts. Dominic Gordon, Fleet Engineer, DOSE Spacearm, arrived from Mars five days past for ground leave in the Los Angeles conclave. Dominic Gordon was to visit DOSEWEX upon the invitation of J.J. Barnes, administrator of that facility. Dominic Gordon had no information regarding possible reasons for his being attacked. He gave a minute and detailed account of the events beginning with his overtaking the convoy of construction vehicles. He did not see his assailant's face, only his legs and hands.

Any friend of J.J. Barnes was treated with great politeness. A friend of the administrator's could even ask questions. No, they had not been able to question the assailant. A passing patrol had seen him deliberately ignite the fuel, and to simplify matters, they zapped the fellow, putting seven slugs into his chest in one-tenth of a second, covering him and the burning vehicle with fire foam split seconds later.

"Your main problem," a nurse told Dom later, after a nap, "is that you inhaled some of the fumes from the foam. You'll have sore lungs for a couple of days."

The nurse was a buxom, motherly, gray-haired lady with infinitely tender hands. He fell in love with her and, on the morning of the third day, walking rather well considering his bandages, he kissed her on the cheek and promised to bring her a carbocrystal next trip back from Mars.

Outside of his room he was met by one of the policemen who had questioned him. They walked down a long corridor in silence, boarded an elevator, exited the elevator. The security man guiding Dom boarded a tube car, and zipped at back-snapping speed to an unknown destination underground where Dom was left to wait in J.J.'s outer office. He passed the time by looking at the left profile of the receptionist. It was a very nice profile and he was in the midst of some interesting speculation when she rose, smiled, and told him that Mr. Barnes would see him now.

J.J. indicated a chair in front of his desk. Dom sat down, leaning his crutch on the chair. There was a hiss and a low rumble as a blockshield closed down around the desk area, putting the two of them in an impenetrable shell.

"You have problems even here?" Dom asked.

"I'm often accused of being overcautious," J.J. said, "but the last time I visited the White House the media had the details of the discussion before I was back at my hotel."

"Name dropper," Dom said. He wiggled, trying to ease the weight off his sore rear.

"Flash," J.J. said, "you're just in from Mars. What was your cargo?"

"Phosphates," Dom said. He knew that J.J. was aware of his ship's cargo, but J.J. had to work up to things. He'd always been methodical.

"Agricultural phosphates," J.J. said.

"Right."

"And the trip before this one?"

"The same."

"Do you ever think about that?" J.J. asked.

"Not a helluva lot," Dom said.

"Why not a cargo of carbocrystals?" J.J. asked. "Or refined platinum? Or gold, or radioactives, or even petroleum?"

"I don't place orders for cargo," Dom said. "If you're trying to give me a lesson in the dynamics of supply and demand, I know why we carry water out to Mars and carry phosphates back. Mars doesn't have enough water and you don't have enough food. You've let the topsoil wash into the oceans and you've ruined what's left by force farming."

"I don't like your choice of pronouns," J.J. said. "You. You, yourself, had nothing to do with using up Earth's resources?"

"I voted for forced family planning in '90," Dom said. "That was the first time I was old enough to vote. I had common sense even at such a tender age. The rest of you didn't."

"I won't bother to claim kinship by telling you that I, too, voted for family planning," J.J. said. "It's enough to say that the rest of the world didn't." He looked at Dom thoughtfully. "The man who tried to burn you was a Publicrat, of course."

"Worldsaver?"

"Party affiliation is public record. Membership in radical and terrorist organizations is not. I would guess either Worldsaver or Earthfirster. The latter, I suspect, since they're becoming a bit more bloody lately."

"Which party leader was he registered under?" Dom asked.

"Our own lovable senator. The gentleman from New Mexico."

"Do you have any ideas yet why he selected me?"

"Not officially. There's nothing on paper to connect you with me or any aspect of DOSE other than the Spacearm. However, in the eyes of the Earthfirsters, any man coming into DOSEWEX is a high-priority target. It's likely that the DOSE vehicle was enough to make you a target. They're getting less and less selective. Just being a spacer is enough to get you killed."

"I know that. I'm used to spending my time in a guarded enclave while I'm on dear old mother Earth."

"And all you want to do is get back into space," J.J. said.

"You know it."

"It's going to take a while," J.J. said. "You're being pulled off Spacearm duty and assigned here."

"Thanks for nothing," Dom said.

Barnes unlocked a desk drawer and put a player on the top of the desk. "I guess it's time," he said. "We've edited out the time lapse between dialogue." He pushed a button.

The sound of deep space filled the room. There was the familiar hiss and crackle of the big emptiness and a wave of sickness hit Dom as he leaned forward. The voices were calm and professional, the voices of spacers, good at their work, a long way from home, linked to Earth only by fragile radio waves.

Houston Control, this is Callisto Explorer. *Zero-nine-three-five hours CSET. Do you read?"*

"Go ahead Callisto Explorer."

"Houston, request check of vehicles in area J-77-343. Repeat. Request check of all vehicles in area J-77-343."

"Hold one, Callisto Explorer. *Stand by,* Callisto Explorer. *U.K. ship* Queen Anne *is nearest you, beyond your instruments at 186 degrees relative reference point two-seven-Baker. U.S.S.R. exploration ship* Khrushchev *relative your position 313 degrees reference point two-nine-Baker."*

"Houston, Callisto Explorer. *Request check bearing relative our position zero-nine-seven, reference point three-three-Charlie. Do you copy?"*

"Got you, Callisto. *Hold one. Nothing there but empty space."*

"Houston, unless your computer is fouled up, there's a bogie out there."

"Callisto Explorer, *repeat please."*

"Houston, we've got a bogie. Closing on the orbit of Jupiter. Estimated speed one hundred thousand miles per second. Repeat, estimated speed one hundred thou-

sand miles per second. Mass estimated at three-zero-zero-zero tons. Repeat, three-zero-zero-zero tons. Houston, we are tracking. Bogie on collision course with planetary mass. E.T.A. outer atmosphere four hours twenty-three minutes."

"Callisto Explorer, *are you filming?"*

*"That is affirmative. We are filming. Is that you, Paul? Listen, this thing is really something. Hold it. Hold one. Yes, we now have visual. What's that, Dell? Let me see. Jesus, that bastard is big. Houston? Put this baby on the ground and you could lay*__ *foot-ball fields inside her length. Estimated length, four-zero-zero yards. Profile cylindrical, tapered at both ends. No visible blast. Possible thrusters at rear. She's closing fast."*

"Callisto Explorer, *where is your bogie now?"*

"She's going to pass behind the planet relative to us in approximately five minutes, Houston. Hold it. Dell, did you see what I saw? Houston, there was some sort of activity aboard the bogie. A glow. It showed on our visual and on the heat scopes. Front and relative the planet. Possible braking activity. Yes, she's slowed slightly. Houston, she slowed faster than is possible. She took off fifty percent of her speed in ten seconds. We're losing her now, Houston. She's getting fuzzy because of the atmosphere. She's not going straight in, but is approaching in an orbital posture. She's fading now and we're getting nothing but the planet."

Dom was sitting on the edge of his chair. He felt an atavistic crawling at the nape of his neck as his hair tried to stand up in an age-old response to the unknown. His pulse rate was up and he was breathing fast.

"Interesting?" J.J. asked, with a wry smile.

"What's a bogie?" Dom asked, not familiar with the term but knowing without doubt that it had been used to refer to an unidentified ship of gargantuan proportions.

"It's antique slang used by some of the exploration ships," J.J. said. "It goes all the way back to the wars of the last century. I looked it up once. There was a fellow named Bogart who played bad men in filmed melodramas. They called him Bogie. In the air wars an enemy fighter was a bad guy, a bogie."

"This ship out there, how do you know it's a bogie, a bad guy?"

"We don't. Later on in time the term came to be applied to any unidentified flying object."

"And is this one still unidentified?" Dom asked.

"Yes."

"It went into the atmosphere of Jupiter?"

"Yes. Two months ago *Callisto Explorer* was pulled off her mission and sent into Jupiter orbit, closer than we've been before. It was almost too close. They used too much fuel getting out of the gravity well and we had to send a rescue ship from Mars. We'll get them, but they're still in space."

"The ship came from outside the system," Dom said.

"Without a doubt."

"And it's lost."

"Not necessarily," Barnes said, tenting his hands under his chin.

"Quit playing games, J.J.," Dom said.

"Listen." J.J. pushed the play button on the machine. Dom heard the great flare of sound which is the background noise of Jupiter. "We have to listen closely," J.J. said.

He heard it then, a thin, weak series of pulses, repeated in the same pattern at intervals of a few seconds. It was difficult to imagine the power of a transmitter which could make itself heard through the great rush of Jupiter's radio output, the crushing radiations of a failed sun.

"Impossible," Dom said. "She'd go right on down toward the core, into a pressure of one hundred thousand atmospheres. Nothing could withstand such pressure."

"We've run this series of pulses through every computer in the world," J.J. said. "We've got the best men in the world working on it, but there's not enough. If someone who didn't speak our language picked up one of our ships sending Mayday he'd be as helpless as we are to figure out what the ship was saying. But we know the signal is amazingly powerful. It has to be to be heard over Jupe's noise. That makes us think she's orbiting just inside the atmosphere. After a careful study of *Callisto Explorer's* film it seems that the ship went in at the right angle and the right speed to establish a stable orbit."

"How deep?" Dom asked.

"Remember that diving hull you designed?"

"It was good to forty thousand feet of ocean," Dom said. "Over a thousand atmospheres of pressure."

"You'll have to more than double those specifications."

"No," Dom said, shaking his head. "You quickly get into the area of diminishing returns."

"We're talking about three thousand atmospheres," J.J. said.

"No way."

"There is a way," J.J. said. His eyes were serious. "There is a way because there's an alien ship down there inside Jupe's atmosphere which is withstanding the pressure."

"If *Callisto Explorer's* observations were accurate," Dom said, "it's faster and bigger than anything we've got, or anything we've got on the drawing boards. It came from outside the system. That means it has either traveled a long, long time, or they've beaten the constant. Either way that puts them far ahead of us."

"Dom, what would be the benefit if we could lift a hundred million people off the Earth and establish them on a life-zone planet of Centauri?"

"If Centauri has a life-zone planet."

"A couple of hundred million more for each new planet discovered," J.J. said.

"It's an old, old dream," Dom said. "And without a sublight drive, that's all it is, a dream."

"What if there's a sublight drive on that alien ship?"

Dom shook his head, thinking of the impossibility of construction of a hull to resist three thousand atmospheres of pressure.

"Do you know how bad it is?" J.J. asked. "We're losing. We're keeping Earth alive by spending the last of our resources flying back fertilizer from Mars so that we can grow just enough food to keep billions of people just above the starvation level. You and I know that space should be more, that it's our last hope, but those hungry people don't see it that way. They look at the space budget and they say that the money could be better spent on Earth researching ways to grow more food, to farm the oceans, to develop the last of the tropical rain forests and to irrigate the deserts. We've been fighting the budget cutters since before the first moon landing. They cut and they slash, and they will win in the end. Every second that passes sees a few more mouths to feed. The Earthfirsters have already put China out of space, and Japan has only a token program. The U.K. is about ready to cave in and give them what they want. Even Russia is having problems. We're fighting now just to hold the current budget, and there's not a chance that we'll win. We're outnumbered. The budget will be cut, and that means an end to exploration and development. All we'll be able to do is make the fertilizer runs. The Publicrats have an absolute majority in both houses, and the President is a Publicrat."

"I don't see—" Dom began.

J.J. waved him into silence. "The President is a good man. Secretly, he's on our side, but he can't fight public opinion. This is an inevitable fact. They're going to cut our budget. First we lost exploration, then development of new programs. The Canaveral site will be the first to be closed, sure as hell. There will be no more building of ships. There's even a move under way to close the Academy, to consolidate it with West Point to save money. You know what that means. They say it's partly for the safety of the students."

"I heard about the last incident," Dom said. "Those kids should have stayed in the campus enclave."

"They didn't, and the Firsters got six of them," J.J. said. "And that seemed to be the first incident in a new wave of terrorism. The bleeding hearts say we can stop the bloodshed by getting out of space. Leave the useless, empty planets alone. Come home to Earth and work together to make it livable. But we're a little late for that. We've used her up, and she's just a shell. We've given her too much of a human load to carry. Too many people, not enough common sense. Do you know that one of the latest terrorist groups kills lumber cutters in the name of freedom for trees?"

J.J. snorted and continued. "Trees, for Christ's sake. Trees have rights. Trees have as much right to live as we. I don't know what they expect us to use to replace the products of the forests, which is the only area where man ever was worth a damn in competition with nature, in that he figured out how to grow trees faster than nature. But they want us to quit killing trees.

They say it's murder and against the individual freedom acts."

"Sounds like the crowded-rat syndrome to me," Dom said.

"We can see that," J.J. said. "They can't. Space is our last hope. We're going to lose that hope unless we can go down into the atmosphere of Jupiter and bring that ship back with us."

"Uh," Dom grunted.

"Dom, you're the best hull man in the service, and, therefore, the best in the world. You're a pressure man. If you can design a hull for a thousand atmospheres, you can design one for three thousand."

"There's the matter of power," Dom said. "We get into impossible figures just trying to furnish enough power for such a ship."

"We've got a power plant. It's new and it's untested, but we've got it."

"The newk?" Dom asked.

"It will be like riding an exploding bomb."

"Whee."

"You're the man, Flash," J.J. said. "You're on the spot. You can pull in anyone you want to work with you."

"Art Donald."

"He's already here."

"Doris and Larry Gomulka."

"Doris is on the way. Larry is finishing a project and will be here within a week."

"That's a good start," Dom said.

"The team you used to develop the deepwater hull."

"Will there be budget problems?"

"Not on this one, Flash. We're going to shoot the works."

"Good, I'll start by charging some work clothes at the company store."

"They'll be deducted from your pay."

"You're all heart," Dom said.

"Oh, we're very generous here in DOSEWEX," J.J. said.

o 3 o

Voices awakened Dom. He was back in the hospital to facilitate dosage of the drugs which were healing his burns so rapidly that he felt, as he came out of sleep, no pain, only an itch under the bandages. His head was fuzzy. He'd taken a sedative to knock thoughts of a three-thousand-atmosphere pressure hull from his mind. He was not ready to open his eyes and face the problem.

"I guess he's showing his age," J.J. Barnes said.

"Plus a total lack of alertness and ambition," said another voice.

"Too much R&R in the big city," J.J. said.

Dom opened one eye. They were standing at the foot of his bed, J.J. in uniform, Art Donald in jeans and pullover. Art was a shattered shell of a man who looked as if he might disintegrate at any moment. He had lung problems. Now and then a few cells would blow a bubble in lung tissue and he'd have a rest in the hospital. His hair was black and lank, his skin pocked by ancient acne, his eyes alert. He was smoking. Art was reckless. At parties he courted blowing a lung by smoking, drinking, and keeping up with the most vigorous on the dance floor. He knew more about metals than any man alive.

"Nice to see you, Art," Dom said.

"You want to get out of bed now?" J.J. said, with some irritation.

"No," Dom said.

"OK, if you don't want to watch a man ride a bomb," J.J. said.

"I'd rather watch a woman do almost anything," Dom said, but he swung his legs off the bed and ducked his head down when it started to spin. A nurse came out of the shadows and attacked him without warning with a pointed weapon. Almost immediately the drug began to counteract the sedative.

He was dressed within minutes and joined J.J. and Art in the hall. There was no conversation in the elevator nor in the lower lobby. It was not until they were riding one of the back-breaking underground cars that J.J. explained.

"We've got a test vehicle waiting about half an astronomical unit out toward Polaris," J.J. said.

"The new power plant?"

"First live run."

"Who's on it?"

"Neil."

Neil was Neil Walters. In space circles it was not necessary to use his last name. "Couldn't ask for better," Dom said.

He had not seen the control facility. It was a miniature Houston, and the duplication amazed him. He began to wonder what else he didn't know about DOSEWEX.

J.J. led the way to a good seat directly behind the contact men and the consoles. Communications were established. It was that old, old simplicity of a pilot talking to the control tower. A mid-twentieth-century airlines pilot would have recognized the form and the cant of the exchange, except, possibly, for a few technical terms. Countdown was underway. Checklists were being followed.

"How many on board?" Dom asked.

"Just Neil."

"High risk?" Dom asked.

"He knows it," J.J. said.

"Is that smart?" Dom asked. "Neil's the closest thing to a hero the space service has."

"Retro switch on," said a controller.

Seconds later, the lag telling of the distance between that enclosed room and Neil Walters' precarious perch atop a new nuclear engine in deep space, his voice came, calm. His voice was always calm. "Retro switch on." Neil rode a test body all the way down into the desert, regaining control just in time to make the crash survivable, and his tone of voice never changed. Only at the last moment had he stopped talking his matter-of-fact reports of engineering gone wrong and computers haywire to perform superhuman things. The cabin padding was impressed with the shape of his body. After a few weeks for allowing bones to knit, he took a reengineered body into the troposphere for a test run.

"It'll be about fifteen minutes," J.J. said. "Want some coffee?" When Dom nodded he snapped his fingers at a cadet.

"J.J.," Dom said. "We've had this engine on the boards for years. How'd you manage to get it built now, when things are tight?"

"We didn't really need it before," J.J. said. "There'd be just a slight increase in velocity, because the harder you push against the constant the harder it pushes back."

"And now that we need it for sheer power, how'd you manage it?"

"By using the last dollar of a little cushion we've

been keeping hidden just for such an ultimate emergency as this," J.J. said. "If we can lift three thousand tons of alien ship out of the atmosphere of Jupiter it will have been worth it."

"And the antis have no idea you're developing the newk engine?"

"Our great director has sworn in front of God and the U.S. Senate's Space Committee that the newk engine has been abandoned and that DOSE never hides anything from our public servants."

"I'm sure that God has forgiven him his untruthfulness," Art said.

"I thought he spoke for God, himself," Dom said.

"And the Senate will forgive him when we bring home that ship," J.J. said.

"Minus ten and counting," the interior sound system boomed.

"So I'm in league with criminals," Dom said. "Do you realize that men have served hard time for lying about something much less expensive to the Congress of the United States?"

"No one lives without risk," J.J. said.

"One thing bothers me," Dom said. "That bogie went into Jupe two months ago and you've already got a hydroplant out in space ready for testing. Am I to believe that you built the damned thing in that length of time?"

"We've had the main components ready for years," J.J. said. "Don't look so grim. It's not as serious as all that. There isn't an agency of the government that doesn't do the same thing. If we all stuck strictly to budget we couldn't even hold the status quo. All the big agencies slip in a few billion here and there for padding in times of need."

"How much padding did it take to duplicate the Houston facility here?" Dom asked.

"What would happen to all our ships in space if some Firster got into the Houston facility with a kilo of plastique?" J.J. asked.

"Aside from a few men getting killed," Art said, "it would kill the program, because Congress would see that as an excellent opportunity to refuse to fund rebuilding the control facility."

"But, dammit, this is just the kind of stuff the antis yell about," Dom said. "I have to admit that for the first time I understand a little about the way they feel."

"Top people know about this place," J.J. said. "Even our friend from New Mexico knows. Aside from the fact that there's no way to hide a place which sends out as much communications as we do, it was good politics for our friend, since it was in his home state and put a few million into the economy of New Mexico. He was one of the most sincere supporters of a duplicate facility, but only behind the scenes, of course."

"Does he know about the hydrogen engine?" Dom asked.

"We hope not. We'll know within a few days."

"How?"

"If the senator from New Mexico knows, the Firsters know. If the Firsters know there'll be a public outcry, at the very least, and at worst an out-and-out assault on DOSEWEX."

"Are they that strong?" Dom asked.

"They're strong and growing stronger every day. I'd say it's fifty-fifty that they'll try a frontal attack on DOSEWEX. It's isolated. On the surface it would seem to be an easier target than, say, Houston or Canaveral, but when it comes right down to it it would be easier to take the Pentagon or Fort Knox. We've got two divisions of space marines within five minutes' jump. We've got the latest weapons. We can fry and slice and implode and burn and freeze and dope and gas a few thousand Earthfirsters with our own security forces."

"But you can't keep them out of the facility," Dom said, flourishing a bandaged foot.

The busy routine went on around them. The mechanical voice of the test coordinator continued the countdown. Dom finished his coffee. The cadet was on hand to take his empty cup.

Under ideal condiitons, every ship in space should be equipped with the hydroplant. If *Callisto Explorer* had had hydropower it wouldn't be sitting out there in space, a dead ship with the air going stale. The hydroplant was not absolutely necessary. The old solid-fuel rockets did the job of exploring the system and running the limited commercial traffic between Earth and Mars. Man could no longer afford expensive programs merely for the sake of progress. The offshoots of space were, almost exclusively, luxury items which the world could live without. Teflon, fabrics, micro-electronics, new scientific techniques, the ability to locate planets for the first time around the nearer stars—not one of those things put food on the table, and when a man is hungry he couldn't care less about a planet orbiting a star so far away that he couldn't reach it in his lifetime in one of the present-day ships.

The harnessing of hydrogen power had eased a few problems. There was plenty of electricity in the industrial countries, but you couldn't use a hydroplant to propel a ground vehicle. The best use for portable hydroplants was in space, and not even almost unlimited power would push a ship past the speed of light and make the stars possible for this generation.

As a spacer, he would feel more secure in the future to know that there was a backup control for Houston. He was even pleased that the hydroplant was, at last, going to be tested. With the world in turmoil, covert actions were the only method available in a continued effort to conquer space before it was too late.

The antis would point out that only five men were breathing stale air in the *Callisto Explorer* as they waited for a rescue ship, while millions were starving. The antis would, if they discovered that billions had been spent to develop a space hydrogen engine, mount war horses and take to the streets to kill the first spacer or cadet they encountered.

Dom didn't like to have to think about such things. He liked to be left free to do his job aboard a good ship and leave the problems of the planet to the politicians. Before J.J. had called him to DOSEWEX, he'd figured that he'd be able to ride the thunderbirds out into space for the rest of his life, even if it meant only the Mars run for fertilizer. Sometimes he dreamed that somewhere, some hidden lab would break the constant during his lifetime, but he had little hope. It would happen, perhaps. He could not believe that man had been created, or had grown, to be confined to Earth and its immediate family of barren planets. If tiny subatomic particles could travel faster than light, there had to be a way to make a ship travel faster than light.

If that alien ship out there in orbit around Jupiter held a key to sublight travel, any deception was justifiable. Even if the mission failed there would be gain. Power would never again be a problem. There would never be a shortage of hydrogen in the universe.

"Almost time," J.J. said.

"Igniter system go," Neil's voice said, thinned by distance.

"I want Neil," Dom said. "I want him to fly the thing."

"He's already assigned," J.J. said.

So it all depended on an untested engine so far away

from the control room that, if it exploded when Neil ignited it, it would take high-resolution telescopes on the orbiting observatories to see the flash of light.

"Preheater on," Neil said.

Now it was all Neil. The countdown was in its last seconds and the time lag did not allow for two-way communication.

"Igniter switch on." The words came calmly, smoothly, space static crackling among them. "Backup igniter switch on."

Even as the words echoed around the silent control room, it had already happened. Neil Walters had set off the bomb under the seat of his pants even before his voice counted: "Four, three, two, one, fire."

Dom could hear the blood pounding in his ears. Fifty people held their breath.

"That is a roger on ignition," Neil's voice said, so calmly. A cheer went up in the control room.

"Acceleration factor point-one-oh-five. All systems go. Stand by for cutoff."

It worked. In spite of strikes in key plants, in spite of demonstrations at space facilities and aerospace plants, in spite of official red tape and the starving millions and social laws against secrecy in government agencies, it worked.

Data was still pouring into the control computers when Dom followed J.J. and Art to a track car which whisked them back to the living complex.

Power was no problem. They would have enough power to jar the earth out of orbit if they wanted to build a plant big enough. With a ship powered by the hydrogen engine there would be more than enough power to grapple on and lift that bogie out of Jupiter's atmosphere and carry it home.

If the bogie didn't resist being lifted out.

If they could build a ship to withstand three thousand atmospheres of pressure without imploding.

If the Earthfirsters didn't mount an attack and do too much damage before the pressure hull could fly.

If they didn't all go to jail.

o 4 o

Doris Gomulka arrived while Dom was watching Art Donald run alloy tests. She came into the lab in her travel clothes, a bit rumpled and dusty, her hair damp with her own perspiration. Doris was a tall girl, small-breasted, thin chest, small waist which flowered into nice hips. She was, in Dom's eyes, one of the more sensuous women of the world, although she made no attempt to exploit it or to enhance her nice face with beauty aids.

Art was about to fire a piece of alloy with a laser. It was an interesting and precise operation which required Dom's assistance. Keeping his eyes on the meters gave him time to recover from seeing Doris for the first time since the water-hull project.

Art burned the piece of metal, and instruments measured the instant of its disintegration and fed the results into a computer. Doris stood quietly until Art was finished. Dom turned and looked at her. He couldn't smile. He tried and the smile wouldn't come. He was feeling it all over again and saying to himself, Look, stupid, the gal is married and happy with it.

"I've got a few problems for you," Art said, with no other word of greeting.

"Right," Doris said. She liked working with Art. He was her kind of scientist. Once a project was under way the rest of the world ceased to exist for Art. He was tops in his field, and she liked that, because she knew, with a quiet and unobtrusive confidence, that she was tops in hers. It had been said that Doris Gomulka could feed random numbers into a computer and make it recite the poetry of Emily Dickinson, if she wanted to waste time on such a project.

Dom had some problems, too. Unlike Art, he could not turn them over to Doris for the solving. His problem was that he was in love, had always been in love, would always be in love with a girl who looked on him as kind of goofy younger brother. And, dammit, he wasn't even younger than Doris.

"Nice to have you aboard again," he said.

"Thanks." She gave him a nice smile. "You're looking good. What's with the feet?"

"A Firster gave him a hotfoot," Art said. "Have you heard from Larry?"

"In this day and time he didn't take his pills and picked up malaria in India," Doris said.

"What we want to do," Art said, having had enough of the civilities, "is take the water-hull formula and run it through with a few alterations."

"She'll want to have a rest from the trip," Dom said.

"With a couple of the new alloys I think we can increase the resistance of the old hull about twenty percent," Art said.

"Art, at least let her have time to wash up," Dom said.

"I don't care if she's dirty," Art said. "Just so she puts on a sterile suit."

"I'm ready to work," Doris said, smiling at Dom.

"The old design can be nothing more than a jumping-off place," Art said. "The Flash here thinks he might be inspired if we go over all the figures again and just add in the progress in techniques which are available."

"It won't come close to what's needed," Doris said.

"We have to start somewhere," Dom said. "I've got a couple of vague ideas. I want to talk them over with Larry before we do anything significant."

"He's no more than three days behind me," Doris said.

"Good," Dom said. "Meanwhile, we'll have time to go over the old design." Doris came to stand beside him as he scribbled on a work pad. Art stood on the other side. Dom gave them a horseback estimate of what an individual hull member would have to stand for a three-thousand-atmosphere hull, using the initials TTA to refer to the hull. Art took his figures and began to run with them, and Doris slipped into a sterile suit and went into the computer room. For them, Dom had ceased to exist and the only reality was the immediate problem. They didn't even look up when he left the lab. If they needed him, they'd remember him and call him, irritated because he wasn't available on a second's notice. He grinned. With that team you never knew who was the boss, and that's the way he liked it. Each member was the best. Each member knew the other members were the best. There was no clash of egos, only a feeling of anticipation and a will to get on with it.

In his office, he told his secretary that he was available only to members of the team and the chief, meaning J.J. He poured coffee and sat in his deliberately uncomfortable desk chair. Desk work bored him. If he had kept the padded, swiveling, seductive chair which came with the office he'd have spent a lot of time sleeping in it.

The office was in top-security country. It was as well protected as the labs and the main control room. The labs were adjacent. They contained everything needed for the preliminary, mainly theoretical work. He could have a full meal from a varied menu at any time of the day or night, and if he desired, it would be delivered to his office or his quarters, which opened off the other side of the office. The office and the quarters were small, but pleasant. They were so well ventilated and so well lit that it was easy to forget that they were several hundred feet underground. In his room were several bottles of his favorite brand of bourbon, a viewer which was capable of receiving topside broadcasts and also offered a selection of taped dramas, documentaries, and scientific film. The music system had been stocked with his favorites, obviously from his preference list aboard his last ship.

A blockshield contained the entire lab-office complex. Communications out were complicated, except for a private line direct to J.J.'s office. It was a good setup for work.

He looked over the reports from Neil's engine tests. The powerplant had worked to design specs, and Neil was riding it home to join the construction team out behind the moon, where the hull would be fabricated. The hull was not even designed yet, but the construction crews were in place. Dom had worked under pressure before, but never like this.

He had been over the engine test data a hundred times, and he knew he was reading it again simply to take his mind off the way she looked when she walked into the lab dusty and rumpled from a trip across the desert by ground car. He kept remembering the Cape and how they had walked under a Florida moon arm in arm, both slightly tipsy. And above all he remembered how her lips flattened and then resisted under his.

And there were other memories, because that kiss under the Florida moon had not been the first. He'd kissed her a lot when they were together in the Academy. They'd even plighted a few troths and made a few plans. Yes, a lot of kisses then, and a lot of tears, openly on her part, secretly on his, when he unplighted his troths and grabbed a chance for an immediate berth on a Mars ship. He grabbed it with both hands and let her hand fall limply from his, leaving her behind. She married Larry Gomulka while he was on his second Mars trip, after he'd told her, as kindly as he could, that his first love was space and that she'd have to accept being number two.

Doris was not the sort to be content with being number two, and she was happy, or she seemed to be, with Larry.

Dom could understand why she didn't want to be the few-weeks-out-of-the-year wife of a spacer, but he could not understand her being happy with Larry. Larry stood two hands shorter than Doris and he tended toward stoutness. He was a small barrel of a man with a protruding stomach and a liking for ordinary beer. He was a smiler. He was everything Dom Gordon wasn't. He was the most unlikely candidate for being Doris' husband, and he was, when Dom came home from that second Mars trip. He was, indeed, Doris' husband.

Well, hell, a good spacer doesn't kiss anyone but his ship, except when on Earthside R&R. He could live with it, or he thought he could until, a little bit drunk, he kissed her under a Florida moon and found her mouth to be as sweet as before, but without the response.

The kiss took place during the early days of the water-hull project. DOSE wanted a vessel to explore the deepest ocean, and Dom was the man. He picked his team, and Doris was the first to arrive. They found themselves with time on their hands. Larry was off, as usual, in some inaccessible place in Africa or Asia. Art Donald was finishing a project in Seattle.

He kissed her, felt a momentary response, then she pushed him away. Marriage was still recognized by some people as an honorable institution. There were people, like Doris, who felt that marriage vows were to be kept. In a world where the vast majority of women took what they wanted when they wanted it, Doris clung to what she laughingly called "middle-class morality."

Dom had never been a pleader. If a girl said no she simply wasn't interested at the moment. She'd be interested later, and if she were not, another would be. It was not egoism or chauvinism on his part, it was just the way things were. He should have backed off when she said no, but he was, he realized, still in love with her. He tried gentle force, pulling her to him. She was strong. She resisted silently.

"Hey, this is Dom," he said. "You know me."

"That's the past, Dom," she said.

"What difference would it make?"

"It would make a lot of difference to me," she said.

"You loved me," he said. "It wouldn't be the first time."

"It would be the first time since I married Larry," she said. Hell, he understood, but he had to preserve his pride. He stood there thinking of things to say. He knew what he should have said.

He should have said, "Doris, I understand. That's the way I thought of you back at the Academy when you were my girl. I admire you for being that way."

Instead, he let his passions guide him, begged her, became a prideless beggar and saw, in her eyes, her loss of respect for him. That made him angry, and he made the situation worse by saying angry things.

"Dom, you are not going to force me to pull out of this project," she said. "I'm interested in it and Larry is interested in it."

"I'm sorry," he said. "I'm being damned unfair. Just put it down to one too many drinks and let's forget it."

"I'd like that."

"It won't happen again."

"Thank you, Dom."

"It wouldn't have happened this time," he said, with one last effort to hurt her, "if you hadn't walked with me."

"That won't happen again," she said.

"Thank you, Doris," he said.

It would have taken a computer and a good operator to figure the miles he'd covered since Florida. There were always girls for spacers, and then she walks into a lab and it's all up front again and, goddammit, she wasn't even beautiful. Her breasts were too small and her hips too wide and she was an intellectual snob and why the hell couldn't he get her out of his mind?

"My boy," he said, "it's a matter of self-control."

He practised self-control. He picked up Art's notes on a new alloy and studied them, and then he was into it, going over J.J.'s specs for a ship which would be impossible to build. They wanted a five-hundred-yard monster with a cargo hold taking up four-fifths of her volume.

"What the hell are we going to do?" he exploded, when he first saw the specs. "Carry the bogie home in her belly?"

"Is that a bad idea?" J.J. asked.

"You're compounding the problems," Dom protested. "You're giving me an impossibility on top of an improbability. How can I build a pressure hull with nothing inside but a huge empty space?"

"You can build as many bulkheads as needed," J.J. said.

"Not if you're going to carry the bogie in the hold," he said.

"Dom, we've got to make everyone think she's nothing but a giant tanker," J.J. said.

"To carry water to Mars?"

"To carry water to Mars. To carry phosphates back. She's too big to be built in secret. We've got to have the backing of powerful men, even if we keep her construction secret from the public. Can you see the senator from New Mexico buying the bogie-on-Jupe idea? Water to Mars he can understand. Even the most rabid antispacers are already half convinced of her economic value, because she can multiply the cargo tonnage between here and Mars."

"But you can't pressurize that much empty hull space," Dom said. "She'll have to be slim. Just about enough space inside the thick hull for a man to walk upright. The smaller and tighter she is the easier it will be to build her to resist pressure."

"She has to be a tanker."

"A tanker or nothing?"

"That's about the size of it."

"That's about the most stupid thing I've ever heard," Dom said.

"I admit that," J.J. said. "But she was sold to the movers and shakers as a tanker. If she can't be built, then we'll just sit here twiddling our thumbs and watch the whole space program go down the starving throats of the breeding billions in Asia and Africa."

Dom started to tell him what he could do with his starving billions, but instead he went back to his office, had a drink, and went back to the specs. In the next few days he developed a sore neck from shaking his head in frustration.

Building a pressure hull was, in principal, a simple matter. Man had been building them for a long time for use in the ocean. In the first of the twentieth-century wars, German pressure hulls, submarines, had almost won a war for a tiny country in central Europe, and the feat was repeated in the second of the wars. Following that, the art of building pressure hulls was refined for submarines designed to travel fast and deep and launch nuclear weapons. The Polaris submarine program, begun in the 1960s, was tied in closely to advances in space. To enable submarines to cruise submerged for long periods, new techniques of communication were developed using ultra-low-frequency transmitters whose signals could be detected underwater. Refinements of those techniques would be used to try to communicate from the dense atmosphere of Jupiter. Moreover, much of the guidance work which was done during the Polaris program was applicable to space navigation. The jump from Polaris to space was a small one.

There were differences between designing a hull for underwater use and for use in open space, but there were also similarities. An underwater hull faces uniform pressure around the entire hull. Thus, it is simple to calculate the exact hydrodynamic load for any portion of the hull. Balance hydrodynamic load against the need for compression inside the hull, and you come up with figures for correct proportioning of the structural elements and the required thicknesses of various parts.

Dom Gordon's pressure hull, which had worked and was still working in experiments and exploration in ocean depths of thirty-five thousand feet, was, essentially, a refinement of the hull design used by submarine engineers since 1918. It utilized a cylinder of circular section, which is another way of saying cigar-shaped, stiffened by ring-shaped frames with a longitudinal spacing of from one-fifth to one-tenth of the diameter. Dom's greatest departure from traditional sub design was in the use of metals which were quite flexible. As the pressure increased, the external loading can cause an entire hull to change shape, thus putting more stress on certain members than on others. The result is excessive localized strain.

When the Polaris submarine *Scorpion* was lost in 1968, the implosion of her hull was heard at great distances by sensitive instruments. The *Scorpion* was operating in a mere ten thousand feet of water, but she was not designed to resist even half of that pressure. That's how much Dom had to go to design a mobile and operable self-powered vehicle for resistance of the one-thousand-atmosphere pressure at thirty-five thousand feet. He did it by holding the size of the cylinder to a minimum and holding the spacing of the support frames to less than one-tenth of diameter. He moved pressure-hull science ahead in a quantum leap, and that leap was small compared with what he was being asked to do now.

Now they wanted him to throw away all of the knowledge gained from experience in the past and build a monster ship which, first, had to fly through space with a negative loading on the outside hull, since space is a near vacuum, then pressurize itself for resistance of not just one thousand atmospheres, but three thousand. In addition, there had to be a slight safety factor. The hull was to penetrate Jupe's atmosphere to three thousand atmospheres, but what if there had been a slight miscalculation and the alien ship lay in three thousand and fifty atmospheres? To put it simply, they'd have to turn around and come home if the hull's limit was a mere three thousand atmospheres, or they could risk becoming a Jovian *Scorpion* and implode.

The more he thought about it, the more it seemed that the task was impossible. J.J.'s tanker requirement compounded the difficulties, and the impossible demands swirled around in his head and left him feeling defeated. He pondered ways of welding seams and the construction of hogging girders, metal fatigue factors, twist and flex, plating thicknesses. The information coming from Art and Doris' work on the newer high-tensile, special-treatment alloys was not encouraging enough.

The first process of putting a ship on the drawing board is to draw an outline of operational requirements. The outstanding and most demanding requirement of the TTS hull was J.J.'s huge cargo hold. A rough layout of the ship, drawn around that hold, made her far too big, even without making allowances for housing other functional requirements. Still, it was possible to make a drawing. After a few tries Dom had a tentative layout for a monster the size of some of the smaller Caribbean islands which could be built, without the TTS features, at a cost just slightly smaller than the national debt. From the impossible, he began to think of compromises, working components into cramped spaces, overlapping where possible.

The entire process was an exercise in futility, for the entire design was based on an illogical premise. It was an excellent example of Gordon's First Law: "Start with crap, end with crap."

Gordon's Law of Agitation also applied: "The more you stir crap, the worse it smells."

He'd been smelling the mixture for several days when Larry Gomulka arrived, a bit yellow from treatment of his malaria but smiling, his round face cheerful, his short body bouncy, his eyes alert, his brain already at work.

Larry Gomulka was a phenomenon. He was, by training, a physicist. He was nowhere close to tops in his field as a physicist. Doris was tops in her field, Art in his, and Dom was the world's leading authority on pressure hulls, but Larry couldn't, or wouldn't, conduct a basic experiment with accuracy. Larry hated tedious, methodical work. His boredom threshold was low. In conversation, Larry jumped from one subject to another, dazing and confusing many plodding types.

Larry had once been offered a very lucrative contract by a textbook publisher to do a series of books titled: *The Poseur's Guide to Physics, The Poseur's Guide to Chemistry, The Poseur's Guide to Astronomy*, and so on down the list of the sciences. He refused, because it would have become a sameness after the first book or two. He was lazy, he loved to play, he tired of a subject easily, he drank too much beer, and he was in top demand whenever there were problems with a project in any field.

Larry Gomulka was a man who knew a little bit about everything. He was omnivorous in his continued learning. He was interested in everything under the sun, and inside the sun, and in the black holes of space. He was a jack of all trades. Had he chosen a field and applied himself to it he could, in all probability, have been a landmark genius. By scattering his interests he was not tops in any specific field, but he was a master at putting things together. Larry was the top problem solver of the century. Not once but many times Larry had walked into a stalled project, talked trash with puzzled scientists who wondered what that clown was doing there, confused them with bad jokes and rapid changes of subject, talking with physicists about the properties of antimatter, the sex urge of the Predicted Moth, and, infuriatingly, without even seeming to try, solved the problem with a simple comment which left dedicated scientists tearing their hair in frustration. Larry had the ability to put it all together, to relate the work of one specialist to others.

Routine work was impossible when Larry was around. When he showed up in the lab, Art and Doris halted their work. The three of them burst into Dom's office. Dom shook hands and examined Larry's round, beaming face and wondered what Doris saw in the man.

Larry ordered in a vile brand of beer, dominated the conversation with wild tales of adventures in India, where the government had paid him well to set up a workable optional method of family planning. Between tales he threw in a question or two about the current project, sometimes not waiting for an answer before burping happily and moving forward into another change of subject.

Dom noted a look of almost maternal adoration in Doris' eyes. He drank too much, laughed until his stomach muscles ached at Larry's outrageous tales. When he finally retired to his quarters he fell into bed with a self-hating groan, disgusted by his overindulgence. He was awakened by Larry's cheerful whistling from the office. He repeated the groan which had been his last waking sound, called for breakfast in the office, dressed, shaved. He took his time, knowing that Larry was at his desk, going over the specifications. He came into the office just in time to accept his breakfast tray. Larry had his feet on the desk. Papers were scattered everywhere.

"Crazy design," Larry said.

"Insane," Dom said.

"Looks damned impossible."

"It is."

"The impossible takes a little longer," Larry said. One of his more irritating habits was the use of glib, trite old phrases. It was just another one of the things you had to forgive if you worked with Larry.

"Coals to Newcastle," Larry said.

"Water to Mars," Dom said.

"Can you carry water and phosphates in the same hull?"

"If you use a lot of water here on Earth to wash it out," Dom said. "Or, you could use the second and subsequent loads of water for agricultural purposes on Mars, or run it through a purifier."

"This hull would hold a helluva sample of the atmosphere of Jupiter," Larry said.

"Thousands of tons of it?" Dom asked.

"J.J.'s not being totally open with you, is he?"

"I don't know. He claims that the ship was sold to the budget makers as a tanker and that if it's built at all it will have to be able to serve as a tanker."

"So, I guess we build him a tanker," Larry said.

"Just like that."

"Damn the torpedos," Larry said.

Dom was beginning to feel better with each bite of his breakfast. "The preliminary layout is neither feasible nor economical," he said.

"The preliminary layout is junk," Larry said. "If you put the entire industry to work on it it would take years just to build the outer hull."

"And there's not much of the aerospace industry left."

"They're making intrauterine devices and toasters," Larry said. "It's too big. We'd have a helluva time just getting it to hold together under its own weight in the gravity of the moon, much less Jupiter. The mission is incompatible with the design. What we need is a small, thin hull built solidly around a minimum crew's quarters and the power plant. Instead, we're thinking of building a pressure hull around a large volume of space."

"Which will have to be pressurized."

"To what?" Larry asked.

"Forty-five thousand pounds per square inch."

"Jesus," Larry said. Then, "Here's how we'll do it. You're hung up in the old forest-and-trees analogy. You're looking on the ship as one unit."

"Isn't it?" Dom asked.

"Why should it be?"

"It's a ship. It's self-contained. It's a unit."

"Why?"

"Pressure on the widest portion of the hull is distributed to every other part of the hull," Dom said.

"So we make that force work for us, instead of against us."

"How?"

"You ever hear of mush bonding?"

"No," Dom said.

"They're working on it at Caltech. Mush bonding. You expand the distance between molecules and inject alloying atoms. The whole thing compresses under pressure."

"I'm listening," Dom said.

"The technique utilizes superheating. Need lots of power."

"There's ample power on board," Dom said.

"We'll run the seams along the length of the hull instead of around it," Larry said.

Dom's breakfast, unfinished, was forgotten. The idea of running welding seams along the length of the hull was damned silly, except that Larry was reaching for pencil and paper. Dom pushed the wheeled breakfast tray aside and leaned over Larry's shoulder.

"The seams slip over each other," Larry said, "as they are compressed. The more pressure you apply, the tighter the bond."

"What's the limitation?"

"Don't ask me, you're the pressure-hull engineer," Larry said.

"Larry, get the hell out of here," Dom said. "Get me

all the dope on mush bonding. Brief it down for me at first. Talk with Art when you're ready and see if the technique can be applied to hull metals."

"I was thinking about taking Doris into L.A.," Larry said.

"Not a chance."

"Slave driver."

"Out," Dom said.

"That's gratitude. Solve a man's problem and he throws you out," Larry complained.

Dom wasn't listening. He was drawing busily. He didn't even hear the door close behind Larry. Two hours later he was putting figures into the computer, because the basic research on mush bonding had been tossed into his lap by Larry. He worked from his desk, communicating with Doris and Art by a closed video circuit. Doris' computers hummed and clacked out possibilities. Art smoked cigarette after cigarette and began to cough.

It came out looking like a ship, with the traditional cylindrical shape, but it would be unlike any other ship ever built. The hull would be constructed of mono-welded longitudinal sections joined by thicknesses of mush bonding. The more pressure was applied to the hull, the more the mush-bonded sections compresed, and the stronger they became. At three thousand atmospheres, the hull would have partially wrapped around itself, compressing the ship into a solidarity held by massive beams across J.J.'s bedamned cargo hold. It would cost billions. It would be huge, but it would work if the mush bonding worked.

After forty-eight hours with little sleep, Dom threw the preliminary recommendations onto J.J.'s desk. He expected an explosion of protest at the cost and the size.

"Mush bonding?" J.J. asked.

"We're going on inadequate data there," Dom said. "The technique needs a lot of testing."

"Get on it."

"After I've had some sleep."

"Take a pep pill."

"I've taken a pep pill," Dom said.

"Take another one."

"I'm not going to be pushed into becoming a speed freak," Dom said.

"We'll pay your bills at a rehab center."

"I'm going to bed."

"Well, put the team to work on it."

"The team is already in bed," Dom said. "I'm going to farm out some preliminary tests to Caltech, where the work on mush bonding is being done."

"That's no good," J.J. said. "Security on a college campus is impossible."

"We can go through a front organization. They won't have to know that the research is going to be applied to a spaceship."

"All right, but make it open. Try to hide the work and you'll have every nut in the country onto it. Do it openly and they won't even notice."

"The purloined letter," Dom said.

"Do your correspondence on your own time," J.J. said.

o 5 o

Officially she was named the *John F. Kennedy*, because it made for good publicity possibilities to name the biggest ship ever built after the President who spent the money to put the first American atop a stick of dynamite and blast him a few thousand feet into the sky. The decision about the name was made at the top of DOSE.

Those who worked on her called her *J.J.'s Folly*, or just *Folly*.

From the beginning, *Folly* was a bear, a real bear. She was a tremendous hole surrounded by a hull. She was the one great example of political expediency. Workmen said good men and good money and good materials were being squandered on a ship which would not be able to lift her own weight out of moon orbit.

Dom made one last attempt to change the design. He did a mockup of an ideal hull for six thousand atmospheres, a sleek, slim, simple hull built to carry a crew of four, a hydroplant, and a grapple. His design could have gone deep into the Jovian atmosphere, locked onto the alien ship, lifted her out, and had plenty of muscle to spare. His design, which would withstand almost double *Folly's* maximum pressure load, would have cost a third less.

J.J. said it was a damned good design, but that it

wasn't a tanker. *Folly* was. He did not call the ship *Folly*, of course, always speaking her full name in awed reverence. He knew what the workmen were calling her and he knew that Dom agreed.

"I know you think it's folly," he said, emphasizing the word, "but you can't imagine the difficulty we had in selling, the idea in the first place, Dom. While we have more behind-the-scenes support than most people suspect, with a lot of elected officials in favor of space development, they can't say so openly. If they did, the Firsters and the Worldsavers would put their own nuts into office, because the man on the street wants butter, not bogies from Jupiter. The very fact that the *John F. Kennedy* is the biggest, most expensive thing ever built is in our favor, because the situation is so bad that only dramatic solutions are attractive. Congress voted us the money because she can carry so much water and so much fertilizer. We couldn't have built her without extra money. Even if we'd had the money squirreled away, we couldn't have built her in secrecy, because it's going to take a maximum effort by the entire industry to do it. She was sold because she can help boost food production and the elected people think that they can get away with announcing the expenditure after the fact on that basis. There are only a dozen men who know why she's really being built, outside of this facility."

"How about that dozen?" Dom asked. "Are they dependable?"

"How can you tell?" J.J. asked, with a wave of one hand. "It's fifty-fifty that one of them will leak to the Firsters before she's finished. If so, they'll try, sooner or later, to destroy her. That's why, other than the fact that she can be built best in space, we're building her out behind the moon. We can screen the moon crews pretty well, because there's only one way to get there, and that's on a DOSE ship."

"Has there been any indication that the antis suspect that a large project is getting under way?"

"It's hard to tell," J.J. said. "There's no more ranting against space waste in Congress than usual, but there have been a few editorials from sources which have, in the past, been more or less neutral. There was a Worldsaver rally in New York last week."

"Yeah, I heard about it," Dom said. "Only twenty-five deaths. A mild one."

"And they got two spacers in L.A. two days ago," J.J. said.

"That I didn't hear."

"We tried to keep it quiet," J.J. said. "The damned fools went out of the enclave. The Firsters used knives, as usual. After what the Firsters did to them I guess they were lucky to be dead."

Dom hadn't given too much thought to security. "Suppose a man wanted to go for a walk in the desert," he said.

"Take out a big insurance policy first. We have constant patrol of the perimeter, but it's impossible to cover all the ground."

"Any unusual activity?"

"No, the usual scattered pickups of individual nuts trying to be heroes, but nothing organized. Not yet."

The *Folly* project continued at a breakneck pace through planning and design. Tests on mush bonding went well. The results of the Caltech tests were fed into the computer, and the word was go. Material for the interior frames went into fabrication. The power plant was being assembled.

In a way it was a pleasant operation to watch, and in a way it was sad. It was nice to be associated with a go-for-broke project. Not since Kennedy set the industry to cracking in the months after the Russians sent up their first Sputnik had there been so much activity in the aerospace industry. Long-disused facilities were being reopened. Prime contractors searched the world for techs and scientists. Anyone who had a skill and wanted to use it, instead of drawing government welfare money, was at work.

Dom was accustomed to working under tight budget restrictions. Once DOSE spent thousands of dollars advising all personnel to use both sides of scratch paper in order to save money. Most scratch pads were advertising handouts from suppliers. He was astounded by his freedom to spend money. If he wanted to get on the horn and put someone to work, say at MIT, he called and sent the bills to J.J. Where *Folly* was concerned, there was no economizing, no compromising quality, regardless of the cost. Her shipboard computers would be the match of anything on Earth, because no one knew how long she'd be in the murky atmosphere of Jupiter and out of touch with the Earth. Nothing would be left to chance. She was to be given every opportunity to fulfill her mission. If it meant spending a few million for a backup system to prevent a one-in-a-million chance of failure, the money was spent.

It was pleasant and it was sad—sad because although it was beautiful to see the whole world working again on a vitally important project and impressive to find that the years of attrition did not prevent the industry from rising to the emergency, the mission could fail. Or that alien ship inside Jupiter might not live up to expectations, the implied promise of providing new knowledge, perhaps even for faster-than-light travel. If the mission failed, or if the knowledge gained from the alien was trivial, the building of *Folly* would be the last act in a drama which began when

Americans were shocked by the beeping sounds of Sputnik I on October 4, 1957.

It was exciting to be a part of a project of such magnitude, and pride extended downward from the top echelon to the lowest construction workers. Many hours of overtime were put in, not to be claimed on pay vouchers.

Throughout the early stages of the project, Dom's team did not see the light of natural day, but worked, sometimes around the clock, in the underground labs and offices of DOSEWEX. There was a feeling of extreme urgency. The faint, distant sounds of the alien ship still emanated from Jupiter, but for how long?

The orders went out from Dom's office to be spread throughout DOSE and the industry. First tests on the power plant were on the nose. The life-support system was being assembled in portable units, to be lifted to the moon when the hull was ready. The computers were being tested by Doris and her team. Hull metals were now being cast, lifted to the moon. Traffic between the Earthside launch sites and Moon Base was the heaviest in decades. Several shuttles per day blasted from Canaveral, carrying beams and bolts, workers and food.

One of the best things about it was the feeling of togetherness of DOSEWEX. J.J., usually aloof and bemused with his problems, would take a moment to pass the time of day with a lab tech. Social barriers were down. It was as if everyone were on the same ship, bound for an uncertain destination and pleased to have company. Nostalgia was the order of the day. One heard the antique, rhythmic, exciting old names, Yuri Gagarin and Gus Grissom, Shepard and Gherman Titov, John Glenn and M. Scott Carpenter and Neil Armstrong taking that first step out onto the dry and sterile surface of the moon, Trelawny on Mars and the

Jones-Edwin probe to the surface of Venus, Mercury and Gemini and Agena and Voskhod One, Radcliff circling the rings of Saturn.

But the one prime subject was *Folly*, frightful *Folly*, so huge, so complicated, so utterly stupid; and she began to take shape, so very, very beautiful, the network of interior bracings lacy and geometric, her size becoming apparent as she grew.

Not one of Dom's crew, with the possible exception of Larry, could have said, without checking dates, how long they had been underground, virtual prisoners of that huge ship which grew, bolt by bolt, weld by weld, in null gravity out behind the moon. Larry could probably have given the time to the hour, because he had performed his main function in the period of one day. He was being used as a contact man. He was the only one who left DOSEWEX at intervals, and he would have said that only those ventures into the outside preserved his sanity. He was bored and he was lonely, because Doris was deeply involved in doing her thing at the console of her computer.

The weeks became months which ran together in Dom's mind. It was almost time to start moving the crew out to DOSELUN when the Earthfirsters made their move, announcing their presence with a single mortar round which fell short of the main gate control tower. That signal round was followed by an all-out assault from two sides of the surface compound.

The sound of the first underground explosion did not register on Dom. The sound did not come from his own complex, and tests of all sorts were always being conducted. He went on with his work until the alert lights in his office blinked flashing red. It still didn't register, as he looked up in puzzlement, until Larry Gomulka stuck his moon face in the door, not smiling for once.

"We're under attack," Larry announced.

"Not now," Dom said absently. "I don't have time for it."

"No choice, old chum," Larry said, smiling now. "Come along to the shelter."

Dom saw to it that his own team, which was vastly expanded by techs, were properly sheltered. He made his way to J.J.'s office, operating the underground rail car by himself. There were space marines in J.J.'s sector. He had to show his identity, and when he was admitted J.J. was not in the office. He was advised by a young cadet to return to his own sector and seek shelter.

"We'll make short work of this, sir," the cadet said. "Then you can get back to work."

Dom walked empty corridors, took an elevator, and bluffed his way into an observation tower. There he found J.J. with a set of binoculars to his eyes.

A small-scale war was being fought at the fences. The automated defense system had caught the first infiltrators in charged areas. Bodies lay side by side along the fences on two sides. Marines had been moved in, and the sound of their weapons was a continuous roar.

"How many?" Dom asked.

"The early estimate was about five thousand," J.J. said.

Dom, with a feeling of sickness, thought he could see almost that many bodies.

"They don't have any really big stuff," J.J. said, as an old-fashioned HE shell exploded a hundred yards south of the tower. "I can't understand it."

"I can never understand stupidity," Dom said.

"The first thing I asked was, where was the main force?" J.J. said. "This is nothing more than a diversion."

"Pretty bloody for a diversion," Dom said, his eyes

trying to move away from the strewn bodies along the fence.

"We have aircraft out. They have not spotted any major force, just the two groups attacking from opposite sides."

It was sheer suicide. What did they hope to gain by attacking a well-defended major facility with hand rifles and a couple of old mortars? A diversion? A diversion from what?

"The computer," Dom exploded, already moving.

"Cool it," J.J. said. "I thought of that first thing. I sent a guard of marines down there on first alert."

"I'll go take a look," Dom said.

The tendency was, after seeing the first interior bracings taking shape, to think of *Folly* as reality, but a few structural members do not make a ship. At the moment *Folly* existed only in the abstract, in Dom's brain and in the brains of Doris and Art, but most of all, she existed in one area, in the circuits of Doris' primary computer. In that machine were months of work and billions of dollars, and no human brain could recreate the information without starting all over, requiring more months. Destroy the computer's memory and *Folly* was a few drawings, a few basic facts in human brains, and nothing more.

The complex where Dom's crew worked and lived was in the most secure portion of DOSEWEX, buried very deep, encircled by other facilities. It was served only by the underground transporation system. Between the hidden labs and the surface world were hundreds of feet of rock and soil. This central core was penetrated by the well-guarded underground in one place and in one place only.

As the car leaped forward, Dom having properly identified himself as a VIP to the marine guards, he told himself that he was worrying for no reason. The stop came quickly. He entered a maze of corridors and trotted toward the shelter, realizing that his months of work had done nothing for his physical condition. He entered the maze to the shelter, designed to prevent radiation entry, and found the inner door standing open. That door was keyed to pass only those whose palm prints were recorded, his among them. He held his breath and peered cautiously around the door.

Death was more immediate here, closer, having come to men and women he knew. Bodies sprawled in grotesque positions, some atop the others. His senses reeling, he counted. This shelter room, assigned to top personnel, was designed for fourteen people. He counted eleven bodies, recounted to be sure, his brain unwilling to admit to even eleven.

Explosive bullets had been used. The floor had a new red carpet, sticky, odorous. He had to move three bodies to be able to see the faces. The eleven dead were technicians and scientists who had been added to the team. Art Donald, Doris, and Larry were not among them.

He left the bloody room and crept slowly down the corridor toward the labs and the computer room. At the first turn he found the bodies of two young space marines. A squad consisted of eight men. With two dead, their weapons beside them, that left six marines of the squad sent by J.J.

Dom picked up an automatic rifle, a short, deadly, spray-shooting weapon, from beside one of the dead marines. He listened for a moment, and in that moment the corridor reverberated to the blast of an automatic weapon. He sprinted ahead and almost ran into death as he rushed blindly into the corridor leading to the computer room. The door to the room flew open and a man in a dark body suit, his face hidden by a black hood, sent a hail of fire toward Dom. Dom flung his body into a side corridor, hearing the splat-splat of explosive rounds as they whizzed past his head, then the thunder of their strike at the end of the corridor. He could not get enough air into his lungs. He had to force himself to move.

His impulse was to hole up, watch and wait, but he knew that he had to move. He went down the corridor to the living area, found Doris' quarters, kicked her door open. The room was empty. He punched the communicator, It was dead. There was an alert button in each room in the complex. Any member of the team could alert security forces with a jab of a button. Dom pushed Doris' private panic button and waited for the flashing lights and ear-piercing sounds, but there was nothing.

The complex was, quite obviously, compromised. It was an inside job. There were eleven bodies back there in the shelter, two dead marines in the corridor. How many of them? How many to kill eleven men and women and two marines and maybe more?

He considered trying to make a break, to seek help from J.J.'s sector. But they had Doris, Larry, and Art. They were in the computer room.

He knew what he had to do, and he couldn't take time to stop and think about it or he'd freeze. He left Doris' quarters and used branching corridors to circle the computer room until he reached a small, flush door which was almost invisible in a wall. His palm opened it. He climbed a narrow flight of steps, palmed open a hatch. The hatch led into the repair and service sections of the vast computer, which towered from floor to high ceiling of the computer room. He entered at mid-level. He was not in sterile suit, but a bit of dust from him would harm the computer less than was intended, he felt sure, by the terrorists. He walked service aisles between banks of equipment in the guts of the computer. At the front, he could look through the facade of the machine through a small port.

There were three bodies lying on the floor, all three in marine blue. A fourth marine was leaning against a wall, a white look of shock on his face, his arm blown half off. The other two marines held automatic weapons and shared the room with five men in dark body suits and black hoods.

Doris, Larry, and Art were in a tight grouping, guarded by the two marines. The five men in the Earthfirster combat garb were unpacking back carriers, stacking neat packets of explosives. Two members of the Firster team were placing charges at the base of the control console. Already detonators were in place and activated. The charges were of a type to be detonated by radio signal from a safe distance. The men in the room below Dom must have known they had little chance of escape, but Firsters were known best for fanaticism. With Firsters, escape would not be the prime objective. They would be more interested in selling their lives dearly, although, in Doris, Art, and Larry, they had very important hostages. It might go either way. They could try to buy their way out by using three of the most valuable members of the TTS team for bargaining, or they might use them as shields in order to take down as many men as possible before they were killed.

Dom had always considered terrorists as the supreme egotists of the universe. The elite suicide squads of Earthfirsters had pulled off some impressive stunts, including the assassination of a President and a head of the defunct CIA, but how could one man, or several men acting in concert, believe that sacrificing a life and then giving their own would change anything? The terrorists just could not see that their actions as individuals, or even as a small, cohesive group, would not affect in any way the inertial rush of society toward devouring itself through overproduction.

The way Dom looked at it, man, as a race, had enough against him. He still had to contend with the basic forces of nature in the form of flood, fire, earthquake, snow, hurricane, volcanoes. Nature was capable of making all of man's bloody past seem amateurish. If natural disaster didn't get you, then nature still got you in the end. Nature seemed intent on killing the race, having instilled a lemminglike breeding instinct that wouldn't stop until starvation got everyone. Man had enough opposition without fighting himself. If death was the only objective, just let old mother nature take her course. Then, as Robert Frost once said, death could come along as a nice surprise.

Dom thought he recognized one of the hooded Firsters as an electronics expert taken onto the team on the recommendation of DOSELUN. The man was good, good enough to have been able to cut off the communication and alarm systems.

The two men placing explosives were moving, shouldering bags of explosives. They started to mount the crawl ladders on the facade toward an entry port on Dom's level. It would take only three or four charges, placed properly, to destroy the work done to date on *Folly*.

Dom concealed himself behind a bank of memory tapes at the entrance to the port. He was wondering if he was not being as egotistical as the Firsters, thinking that he, one man, could stop seven armed and well-trained terrorists. He was a spacer, a hull engineer. He'd had a few weeks on the combat range back at the Academy, and he'd taken hand-combat courses as a part of keeping physically fit. But he was no trained killer. In his favor was the fact that he was still in fairly good shape, in spite of the months of desk work.

And he was quick. One of the things against him was the fact that he'd never tried to kill a man before.

The human head is a tough nut. It's built to survive blows which are astonishingly powerful. Dom, knowing this, overdid it. He swung the stock of the rifle with all his strength. Both of the Firsters had entered the bowels of the computer and moved past him. The head of the trailing one burst, making quite a mess which would have to be cleaned up before the computer could be functional again. Dom was moving fast, the backward swing of the rifle taking the second man as he turned, a gout of blood spurting through the nasal holes in the dark hood. Dom's reaction time, fastest ever recorded at the Academy, was aiming a second blow at the falling face and white teeth flew and there was more blood and the stock squished down to be sure.

He was still crouched. There was no sound of alarm from below.

He was surprised at his lack of reaction to having killed two men. He was panting as he looked for signs of life. The second man jerked a bit and tried to breathe through the pulp which had been his face, but then he was still. Such men lived only to be killed, he thought, and he'd obliged them. The original mistake in handling terrorists was in not recognizing the basic fact that terrorists considered themselves to be expendable and this made them less than human, to be expended by society as forcefully as possible.

But he was not judge and jury. He was not, after all, hardened to killing. Shock came to him as the second man's legs did a dying tattoo on the padded floor. And there were five more of them down below. Also below were Art, Doris, Larry. All three would die, without mercy, if he weakened, shocked by the quantity of blood in a man's head.

He stepped over a body and looked out the port. They were waiting below with an alert but stoic patience. One of the terrorists was smoking. Dom calculated the chance of taking all five of them with a blast from the port. No way. The shots would also take one or more of his three friends. He moved back, jerked the mask from the ruptured head of the Firster who had been first to die. He cringed at the wetness, but fortunately the blood was mostly on the back side of the mask. He took a deep, shuddering breath and pulled it over his head. He stuck his masked head out of the port and made a hissing sound. They all looked up at him. He pointed to a hooded man and made a come-up-here motion. The man shouldered his weapon and came scampering up the ladder.

The plan was to have them come up one or two at a time, but it didn't work. The man on the ladder saw the bodies of his companions and started to yell out. Dom clubbed him. He fell, half in, half out of the port. A burst of explosive rounds shattered the facade of the computer. Dom leaped to the view port and swept the room below with rifle fire, careful not to fire too close to the tight group of Art, Doris, and Larry. The two traitor space marines went down along with two of the Firsters.

Art Donald, moving with surprising swiftness, jerked Doris down, fell atop her behind a subconsole. They were out of the line of fire. Larry was not fast enough. He was seized by one of the two remaining men. The other one moved to stand on the other side of Larry, the three of them up against the control console below Dom and out of his line of fire. One of the terrorists began to shoot up the face of the computer with methodical thoroughness. Both of them stayed close to Larry. Dom was unable to fire. He had to dodge the fire which swept across the facade. The explosive missiles did not penetrate, but they sent small pieces of shrapnel flying.

"You can't get out of here alive," Dom yelled. "You can live, if you choose."

In spite of the fact that terrorists were not executed, but merely confined as if the authorities wanted to keep them healthy until their friends could kidnap an important official to trade for the freedom of the imprisoned ones, they rarely surrendered.

"Put down your weapons," Dom yelled.

A new burst of fire was the answer. When it died down he looked out the port. There had been a change in strategy. Having failed to destroy the memory banks, they would now try to damage the program by killing three important people. He watched helplessly as one of the surviving terrorists pulled out a grenade and lifted it toward his mouth to pull the pin. The grenade would take out Doris and Art, and they had their hands on Larry. Dom had a choice. By leaning out and pointing his weapon down he could take them, but it would mean sweeping Larry with the deadly explosive bullets.

The situation moved toward a point of no return in slow motion, for Dom could not bring himself, not even to save Doris and Art, to kill the smiling little man who was sandwiched between the two Firsters. He couldn't do it. There was nothing he could do except cry out a protest.

But Larry Gomulka was a problem solver. It was his specialty. He, too, watched the movement of the grenade upward toward the white teeth of the Firster, and the direction of the man's gaze revealed his intentions.

"Stay down," Larry yelled, as he leaned forward and calmly flipped the manual exploder on one of the charges planted on the console. All Firster explosive devices were equipped with manual detonators. Public suicide was a popular hobby among the Firsters, and they liked to take people with them.

Dom felt the face of the computer blow inward, heard the concussion, felt himself falling. He was moving as he fell, scrambling to his feet as the echoes tore at his eardrums. Art was moving, trying to lift a portion of the console off his back. Doris was under him, screaming. Dom could see her face. He dropped the rifle. It struck what was left of a body and rolled to make a solid-sounding thunk on the floor. The body in the hatchway had been blown forward by the blast and was minus a leg. The console was a ruin, and a hole had been blown into the base of the machine. An armless torso rested against the remains of an overturned subconsole. It was not Larry. The chest was too big. The black body suit had been blown away to expose strong, young chest muscles. Dom heaved on the console, and Art was trying to stand up, shaking his head. Doris was swallowing, trying to restore her hearing. Dom helped Art to his feet and left him leaning against the shattered computer face. He lifted Doris.

"Are you all right?" he asked, his voice sounding faint. His ears still roared with the explosion.

"I can't hear you," she said. She spoke loudly. "Larry's dead?"

Dom nodded. "He saved your life," he mouthed at her.

Her face seemed to melt. There were no tears, just a heaving of her chest and strangled sounds from her throat.

The outer door burst open and space marines dashed in, looking young and impressive and futile. Dom recognized the young cadet officer who had assured him that the marines would handle the situation swiftly.

Now came the reaction. He trembled. He felt as if

he was going to vomit. He never wanted to hear the name *Folly* again. Whatever she was worth, she was not worth the life of one small, slightly overweight, beer-drinking, smiling man. He leaned backward, almost falling before his hips found the edge of the shattered console. Doris put her hand on his arm and looked at him.

"He kept them from destroying the information banks," she said. For a moment Dom thought she was talking about him, wanted to laugh, but then he realized that she was thinking of Larry. "He saved the project," she said.

Dom knew that she'd get it straight in her mind later. For the moment, it didn't matter what she thought. Larry had saved something far more important to him than the information in the computer. He had saved the life of the woman he loved and the life of a friend.

o 6 o

At one end of the room thick plastic ports gave a view of the stars, bright, undimmed by atmosphere, hard and sharp points of light in a pitch-black sky. Among a small group of people at the far end of the room, so that the stars were not visible to them, Dom stood in full dress uniform. Doris, too, was in the parade dress of the service. Art Donald was, in fact, the only civilian present as a four-star admiral presented Larry's medal to his widow. The ceremony was being televised live to Earth.

When it was over and the admiral was on his way back to DOSEAST in Washington, Dom watched Doris gulp a full ounce of raw scotch.

"I don't want it," she said, looking down at the small gold medallion in her hand.

"I think I know how you feel," Dom said.

"Larry would have laughed his head off at this," she said.

"Yeah."

"He would have said, never was there a more unlikely candidate for the Space Medal of Honor." She smiled faintly, but there was no joy in the smile.

"No man ever deserved it more," Dom said.

"Amen," Art said.

"Is your life worth so much?" Doris asked bitterly. "I don't value mine that high."

Art choked on his drink. "I didn't mean it that way."

"Oh, Art, I'm sorry," she said. "It's just that I think it's all so funny. So very, very f-f-funny."

"Easy," Dom said, putting his hand over hers.

"There's no way Art could have known that we, Larry and I, have talked about this very sort of thing," Doris said. "He said heroism, especially the sort which entails the ultimate self-sacrifice, is one of our more cherished traditions, beginning with the Spartan boy who let a fox or a rat or something gnaw out his guts for some reason. Then the good soldier throws himself atop the grenade to save the lives of his buddies at the expense of his own. Isn't it very strange, he would say, how the top medals, the Congressional Medal of Honor and the Space Medal of Honor, are so often awarded posthumously?"

"I think if you'd asked him how he really felt he would have explained that top medals are awarded posthumously to show our great regard for individual life," Dom said. "When a man gives all he has, his life, for a buddy, or his country—"

"Then let's give the Congressional Medal of Honor to all of the Earthfirsters who commit suicide," Doris said.

"It isn't the same," Art said, weakly.

"No, it isn't," Doris said. "Because they're not dying for what we happen to believe at this particular time."

"Do you doubt that Larry died for what he believed?" Dom asked. He knew she was on the narrow edge, and he thought perhaps it was time someone or something pushed her over. She had submerged herself in her work following the attack on DOSEWEX, first in repairing the computer and then in the project.

"But that's it," she said, her face puckering as she looked at him. "Don't you see? That's it." She had to swallow and work her mouth before she could continue. "If I could believe that he did it for the project, for the world—"

"He had that in mind, too," Dom said. "You know how fast his mind worked. He measured all of it, the project, the effect on the future. He put all of it into his mind as a problem to be solved and he solved it. The solution called for him to punch a button on a detonator." He was doing it deliberately. She had not cried, to his knowledge. Not once had he seen her show emotion, not until she was holding a small piece of gold in her hand.

Art, not realizing what Dom was trying to do, looked uncomfortable. He tried to get Dom's attention, to tell him to be quiet.

"He added it all up," Dom went on. "He added in the lives of Doris Gomulka and Art Donald, the ship, the alien out there in the atmosphere of Jupiter. He balanced all the factors against the life of Larry Gomulka, and it evened out. And if you try to take out even one element of that decision, the life of Doris Gomulka, then you're robbing Larry of his last successful problem solution. You're saying that he failed, because he had it figured wrong and his death is not evened out by your being alive and the project continuing. If your life isn't worth the value he assigned to it, he gave more than was gained."

He was still holding her hand. She tried to pull it away. She was breathing hard.

"Larry died so that, among other things, you might live. You have to admit that, Doris. Give that to him. Don't try to take that away from him."

It came out of her in an agonized, low-pitched wail, a river of sadness. She made no attempt to cover her face. Her lips distorted, her eyes closed, squeezing out tears. Her face was dramatic in its expression of pain, and the sound of her sobbing was too much for Art. He left the scene. She gulped air and sobbed. Dom led her gently toward the couch and pushed her down. Her hands were clenched at her sides. She wept with great gusto and noise, not neatly, not at all ladylike. There was wetness and huge gulpings and hoarse, grating noises and grunts of pain.

When the worst was over he positioned her on the couch and covered her with a blanket. He left her still weeping, but more quietly.

As he changed in his own quarters and went into the lock to don the heavy suit, he felt a little misty-eyed himself, for Larry would have enjoyed the sight of *Folly* hanging up there in space. He wondered if he would have been fast enough and decisive enough to do what Larry had done if he'd been in Larry's place. He didn't know. But he would never again ask himself if Larry's death had been worthwhile.

He took a jumper up to the construction site. The plates were going on over the interior skeleton. Monowelding required the near vacuum of space. He could see miniature stars where the welders were at work. It was all done in an eerie silence in the airlessness. The stars were a quiet audience.

A good spacer has a celestial clock of sorts in his head. He knew, as he watched from a short distance, the relative position of the planets in their orbits. Mars there, finely visible. Jupiter was hidden, if he had been at a telescope, behind the bulk of the moon.

But the signals still came. Their strength was undiminished, not quite strong enough to be easily detected from Earth. They were being constantly monitored from the moon and from ships in space.

The new freedom of spending which was the hallmark of the project extended outward from the construction site in an expanding fan of beneficial largess for the entire service. The necessity of monitoring the signals sent ships out, and while they listened, they did useful work which had been planned but unfunded for decades. Once again the gathering of space data was a going industry. Men practiced science for the sake of science, just to scratch that persistent human itch for the knowledge of what lies over the next hill.

A ship monitoring the signal from Jupiter could be taking magnetic measurements or aiming shipboard telescopes out beyond the system or picking up asteriod samples or doing any one of hundreds of small research projects which would add to man's knowledge. Even the critics were sold on the extra research in order to make the most out of the necessity of having ships in space.

Dom's presence on the moon was not essential. His work was done. But it would have taken an act of Congress to get him away, even if he did not participate actively in putting together the Tinker-Toy construction which would become the *John F. Kennedy*. (If he thought of her as *Folly*, he added the word *"Grand"* in front of the epithet.) There were ongoing crises and decisions to be made, but he could have made them from DOSEWEX or DOSEAST. On the other hand, Doris was valuable and Art Donald's team was needed to run a series of tests on construction as it went into place.

She grew rapidly. There wasn't another building project under way anywhere in the world. The department was concentrating all its manpower and most of its available money on the *Kennedy*. She was the topic of conversation wherever DOSE people worked, from Earthside to the last picket ship out near the mass of Jupiter.

The grandeur which was a ship took shape in her own element with the pocked moon and the blackness of space as her backdrop. It made for a serene and beautiful picture. Sitting in a jumper five thousand yards from the *Kennedy*, it was difficult to imagine the conflict going on down there on that blue-and-white ball which was the home planet. There, governments were being changed. Fighting varied from savage and random acts of terror by the Firsters to the highly charged atmosphere of the Senate, where radicals were locked in combat with the outnumbered men who believed in a future for man which did not entail buttoning up and toughing it out on the home planet.

For weeks a debate raged over the battle of DOSEWEX, where thirty-two hundred Earthfirsters died. The ruling party, the Publicrats, received the brunt of an attack from rabid, self-confessed Firsters and Worldsavers. Liberals wept openly on the Senate floor as they bewailed the mass slaughter of humanity at DOSEWEX, and, in their zeal against the death penalty for terrorists, they called loudly for the pitiless execution of all those responsible for the slaughter of innocent terrorists who were merely using their First Amendment rights to express dissatisfaction with space policy.

Only once did a courageous man stand up to remind the Senate that two dozen civilians died at DOSEWEX, along with over a hundred space marines. He was hooted into silence. On the way to his fortified apartment, he was attacked by a teenage Firster girl in a sexy little dress which concealed a bomb in an oversized bra. The bomb ruptured the brave senator's left eardrum and killed two of his bodyguards. Thus were courageous and commonsense views silenced, without regard for First Amendment freedoms.

It was almost as if the majority of Americans felt guilty for taking the government's cradle-to-the-grave security at the expense of individual freedom and wanted to be punished by the Firster knife or bomb. Overpeopled, underfed, the country was one teeming warren of interconnected big-city heaps where people suffering the traumas of crowding seemed all too eager to die and saw no promise in tomorrow.

Earthside was such a turmoil that there was no ground leave. The limited facilities of the moon were taxed by the construction crews, and spacers in from Mars or the Jupiter surveillance run sometimes had to spend their ground time aboard ship. Their bitchings were surprisingly good-natured, for they could see the *Kennedy* as she grew.

Dom spent a lot of time with Neil Walters, who would test and pilot the *Kennedy*. Although he was older, Neil was a perpetual boy of twenty-five in appearance. He stood six-four and was topped by a mop of blond, curly hair. He had deep, laughing blue eyes and a classical angularity of face which went with his daring and his reputation. He liked talking about flying only slightly less than he liked flying. He set out to learn the *Kennedy* from the smallest component upward. He was good company, for the *Kennedy* had become Dom's main reason for living.

When she flew, Neil would be in command. He had a sharp mind, and Dom never had to explain even the most complicated technical details. In fact, Neil posed questions which put Dom back into the lab, Doris with him at the keyboard of a computer, to check and recheck. Neil's questions were basic and penetrating. They caused Dom to check all the important calculations and the thinking which went into the revolutionary concept of the folding hull. Dom discovered nothing serious wrong, but he did make slight changes here and there.

Neil's main criticism of the plan was that it would be impossible to test *Kennedy's* hull under pressure.

"Either it works when we get down into Jupe or it doesn't," Dom said.

"Well, it only has to work once," Neil said, with a wide grin.

"We'll be reading the stress on the hull as we go down, reading it carefully and following it all the way," Dom said. "We can always turn back if something begins to give."

Neil laughed. "One good thing about this one. If something goes whango I might have time to spit right in the designer's face before I check out."

Neil was stimulating, but not even talking with Neil could fill all the hours. There was not a lot to do on the moon. Drink was expensive, because there were no distilleries on the moon and booze was a luxury item not included in rations. Dom spent a lot of time in the observatories, He played some bridge. He explored a bit, but once you've seen one acre of the moon's surface there is a sameness. One crater is like every other crater, just a bit bigger or smaller. He also did a lot of reading. But still the days dragged and the weeks were endless and the months were eons. The ship grew, and that was the main pleasure, just going out there to see what work had been done in the past twenty-four hours.

It was interesting when the monowelders began to join the mush-bonded collapsing seams to the plates. It went just as predicted, with no problems.

Doris had her work. She kept busy, finding time for dinner with Dom only occasionally. When they were alone Dom was careful to stick to business and keep the conversation away from personal things. After that bull market of weeping on the day she received Larry's medal, she could talk about him without pain. It was no longer necessary to remember not to mention Larry, because she often did. As if Larry were merely off somewhere on one of his jaunts, she'd say, "I wonder what Larry would think about that?" He lived in her memory, but he did not become an obsession. Dom suspected that her grief was not totally spent, but it was not a festering sore. She could laugh at a joke, be sentimental about a love song, muse over her memories, all without giving the outward appearance of a perpetually grieving widow.

J.J. made regular trips to encourage, investigate, cheer, and urge on. He was on the moon the day air was pumped into the hull and for the first time workers could operate inside the *Kennedy* without life-support gear. Work on the fittings and finishings began to go faster. J.J. sat in the pilot's seat and examined the instrumentation spreading before him.

"I'll have to take a refresher course," he said.

"For what?" Dom asked.

"To be able to fly this mother."

"You?"

"I'm copilot," J.J. said.

Dom considered the advantages and the disadvantages of that. "I can't think of anyone I'd rather have," he said.

"Bless you, my son," J.J. said airily. "It will be understood, of course, that I am senior only in rank. In ship operations I'll be second in command to Neil and you, and only you will have the final say about safety."

"Bless you," Dom said.

J.J. looked ahead, out the front port. "Flash," he said, "it's all going to be in your hands there on Jupe. We're shooting the works, all of us, on this trip, but there's no need for us to die needlessly. If it works, you'll get credit for it. If it fails, no one will ever be able to tell you I told you so. But remember, if we lose, if it doesn't work, the whole silly damned human race is the prime loser."

Dom had no comment to make on that.

o 7 o

Dom was having dinner with Doris the night J.J. called from DOSEWEX to order him to report to DOSEAST to testify in the matter of Larry Gomulka's death.

It had been a nice evening. For once, Doris had no pressing problems involving the *Kennedy*. The shipboard computers were being installed and the components which were already in place were working beautifully. She was relaxed. She was ten pounds lighter than she'd been when she walked into the lab at DOSEWEX with travel dust still on her clothing. She was slim and elegant in her uniform. The lines around her eyes, which had appeared after Larry's death, were fading. She looked younger.

The evening came about by accident. Dom happened to be walking past the lab when Doris decided to call it a day. Dom offered to buy her a drink and she accepted. They sat in the canteen and listened to music which was more for background than for listening, both of them comfortable without talking. When they did speak it was shop talk.

Dom suggested that they call Art and have a threesome for dinner. Doris agreed, and went to make the call.

"He's tied up," she said. "Have to be just the two of us."

"I'm hungry enough to eat Art's dinner, too," Dom said. "Where? Here? The food's not bad."

"I'd like to be able to hear myself chew, or think, or talk, or whatever," Doris said.

"That rules out the cafeteria as well," Dom said.

"I'll make the supreme sacrifice," Doris said. "I have just two steaks left from the last ration. Real steaks."

"Greater love hath no woman," Dom said, rolling his eyes.

"I believe in buttering up my boss," she said.

"I'll pay you back, swear." He held aloft a Boy Scout sign.

"Put it in writing."

"You question the honor of an officer and a gentleman?"

"I learned to question the honor of officers, male officers, when I discovered that the chief engineer on my first ship had altered the combination to the palm lock on my cabin door," she said.

Dom grabbed a napkin and wrote: "I owe Doris Gomulka one real steak." He gave her the napkin.

"You didn't sign," she said.

He jerked the napkin back and scrawled his signature. "You are a person with very little trust."

"Not where steaks are concerned."

Doris' quarters were on the frontside. Earth was almost full, low on the horizon. The richness of her, blue and white, made her a jewel in the sky.

"My God," Doris said, halting as they entered to see the great living globe hanging there in the window.

"It's always new, seeing it like that."

"So beautiful," she said. "You know, I'd like for all of them to be able to see that, to see how small and goddamned vulnerable she is, hanging out there. Maybe they'd think a little more clearly. Show them a closeup view of Mars, or Mercury, worlds totally inhospitable to man, and then show them that. How can anyone fight over anything so beautiful?"

"Actually, I guess, in a way, we're the new nobility, so few of us have seen that."

"Thank God you can't see what we've done to her from up here," Doris said. "Strip mines and underground nuclear tests and radioactivity in the air and sewage in the oceans. And she still manages to support all of us, after a fashion."

"And only now and then strikes back with an earthquake or a drought," Dom said, grinning.

"OK, cynic, you make the salad."

The salad greens were grown hydroponically on the moon and were plentiful. The steaks were great treasures and were strictly rationed.

Doris put on a couple of antique music tapes, the sound turned low. They talked small talk, working side by side in the kitchen, having a pre-dinner drink. The steaks were cooked very, very carefully.

Doris ate with an eagerness which was fun to watch. She ate like a hungry man, no talk, no nonsense. Finished, she wiped her lips on her napkin and breathed a deep sigh of contentment. The few dishes were handled quickly, the washer turned on, recycled water doing the job. Doris poured brandy.

Earth was thirty degrees high, and to see all of her they sat side by side, facing the viewport, silent, the music soft and nostalgic. Dom had never felt better. The ship was coming along. The steak had been delicious. The brandy was one of the better synthetics. Doris leaned back, the long line of her throat a delicate curve. Her hair fell into sort of a frame for her face. She was wearing the short uniform. Her long legs were tanned by hours in the exercise room. She swung her crossed leg in time with the music.

There was something about the music which was very familiar, and they both noticed it at once. She had been humming quietly, now and then voicing a phrase, and he was aware of her as a woman. He had to clear his throat and look away.

"It's been a long time since I've heard that one," she said, as the song ended. It had been their song. They'd danced to it many times during the Academy days.

He stood. He had to move or he'd do something which they'd both regret. He stood beside the port, and Doris came to him. As she passed the player she turned the volume up slightly. Another old, familiar song was playing. He sensed her nearness, felt her brush against him.

"We danced a lot to that one, too," she said musingly.

He looked down at her. Was it possible that she felt the same thing he felt? She was humming again, swaying her body to the music, looking up and out to peaceful-looking old Earth up there in the sky.

The music changed to upbeat. "Hey. I can't stand that," she said, putting down her glass. She took Dom's glass and put it down and lifted her arms. He took her hand and began to dance. He got the feel of it after a few steps and they reminded each other of the old steps, laughing as it came back. Fads in music and dancing changed so fast that Dom couldn't always remember which type of dance went with which, but Doris was an authority.

The music went soft and slow. Dom felt the warning bells go off as she came into his arms, put her cheek to his, and began to dance, close, dreamy. She was a perfect fit, almost as tall as he, a size to cuddle in his arms. He had to remind himself that women looked on dancing as something almost impersonal. To Dom, slow dancing was hugging set to music. Women seemed to attach less sexual significance to dancing, but to Dom body to body while swaying with the music was just as thrilling as body to body under any other circumstance. Ah, she was good in his arms, and he didn't turn loose as one song ended and another began. He turned his head slightly and kissed the smooth, soft curve of her neck. She sighed.

It seemed to happen naturally. Lips to lips, they stopped dancing and the kiss went on for eternity and there was promise in her response. He had wanted that kiss for so long, dreaming of it for all of the long years since he said goodbye to her and went off on his first trip to Mars.

"Stay down," Larry yelled, bending quickly to trigger the detonator.

Dom broke the kiss, pushing her away. "I'm sorry," he said. "Earth got in my eyes."

"I know," she whispered, leaning toward him. "I wanted you to kiss me."

His heart leaped. He moved toward her. She put her hands on his chest. He looked into her eyes in question.

"I'm not saying no," she said. She looked away, biting the corner of her lower lip in thought. "I want to be sure to say this right. First, it's been a long, long time since you kissed me like that, and I liked it very much."

"I hated it." He grinned.

"But I think you were feeling the same thing I can't help feeling when you pushed me away," she said.

"I was thinking about Larry," he admitted.

"Yes," she said.

He turned to face the port and watched a surface crawler moving across his field of vision. He was still thinking about Larry. He tried to view the situation from Larry's viewpoint, thinking of him as being out there, somewhere, able to look back and see what was happening. Problem: a young widow. Solution: a man, but not just any man, a man who would love her and cherish her. He turned to look down at Doris' profile.

"Would you think I was being silly as hell if I said I think Larry would approve?" he asked.

"No," she said. "He knew about you. If he was ever jealous of my, uh, having given myself to you first, he never said so."

"I'd like to know what you think," he said.

"I've been intimate with two men in my life," Doris said. "And I loved you with a big love once, damn you."

"I've loved you since the first time I saw you," he said.

"But you loved space more."

"Guilty, I suppose. I'm older now. We're together."

"There's that to think about," she said. "We've got a job ahead of us. We're going to be in crowded quarters for months with others."

"There is that," he said.

"The lady is not saying no," she said.

"Just wait a while," he said. "We could get married."

"We could."

"But you're not so sure?" he asked.

She sighed. "I feel like a silly and indecisive teen-ager."

"Can you love me, again?"

"Oh, I've always loved you, too. As a young girl loves in the deepness of first love, as a sister loves, as a friend loves."

"That wasn't a friend or a sister kissing me a few minutes ago," Dom said.

She laughed. "Dom, if you want to make love to me

you'll find a most willing participant." She looked him straight in the eyes. "Do you want to?"

"Yes." He shrugged. "All right, dammit, you must have infused me with your middle-class morality and your sense of responsibility. You are infuriatingly right and I hate you, you smart-assed female."

"There will be time," she said. "When we get back from Jupiter."

"Years and years," he said, kissing her lightly and pushing her away as she went molten in his arms.

Within twenty-four hours he was on a shuttle. He carried with him sworn depositions from Art and Doris, who could not be spared from the *Kennedy* project. Neil was supervising in-place static tests of electrical systems and the power plant. He resented being pulled away, leaving the team working, but he went down, roaring into the muggy atmosphere, noting double security at the Cape. He flew a carefully guarded jet to Washington.

The hearing was held deep inside the main DOSE installation outside the city. Dom made his statement and answered questions. Nothing new came out of the piles of paper which were the result of the hearing. However, Dom was reminded of the ability of the Firsters to penetrate the most secure installations.

Since all of the inside team of terrorists had been killed, there were unanswered questions. No one could suggest how the explosives were smuggled into DOSE-WEX. It was possible that the traitor space marines could have done it, or one or more of the technicians who were Firsters.

J.J. expressed the doubt. "We are reluctant to admit that there might be high-level traitors among us. You and I, Dom, are more or less sensible men. We can think that it took someone with more clout than techs or marines to place so many Firsters on your lab team."

"It was your office which cleared each one of them," Dom said. They were having a meal in a secure hotel while Dom waited for a flight back to the Cape.

"My office," J.J. said, "consists of more than just a room. It involves a couple of hundred people. They've all been investigated backward and forward, and I wouldn't bet my life on the loyalty of more than a handful of them. Some minor clerk somewhere could influence a screening with a deft shuffling of papers. Someone in higher authority could bring pressure on people elsewhere to get a particular man into DOSEWEX. Personally, I don't think the raid on the computer could have been planned without someone of at least administrative rank pulling strings, and that opens such a vast array of possibilities that I don't dare start an investigation. One thing for damned sure, we're going to have to be one hundred percent sure of every person aboard the *Kennedy*."

"I should hope," Dom said.

"We're sure of so few," J.J. said.

"Me, you, Art, Doris, Neil," Dom said.

"Are we sure of all of them?"

"If we're not, we're in so much trouble we might as well give up," Dom said. "I've been thinking a lot about the crew list, J.J. In addition to the basic five, it calls for a cook, a powerplant engineer, a survival-systems specialist, and a medical tech. I think we can weed the list down. We can take turns with the cooking. We can risk going without a medical tech. We've all been around enough to have learned basic medicine, first aid, treatment of minor ailments. If something major comes up a medical tech might save a life, but that's a risk I'm willing to take. That would leave us needing only two people in addition to our hard core of five, an engineer and a survival-systems specialist."

"I've been thinking along the same lines," J.J. said. "Any suggestions for the two we need?"

"Paul Jensen and Ellen Overman," Dom said.

"You've worked with both of them, I think."

"I've been on two tours with Paul. He's a damned fine engineer and he hates radicals of all sorts. The last time I was in touch with him he was going to ground on Mars to supervise the installation of a new generator. He said he was doing it because he got so goddam mad each time he came back home and saw what the world was coming to."

"He's still there," J.J. said.

"Ellen was with me on the Saturn expedition and on one Mars run. She's good at her job."

"I'll start the checks on them," J.J. said. "What about Ellen? I know Jensen, but I know her only from her service record."

"She's the independent type, the complete woman. I don't know a lot about her politics, because I wasn't that close to her."

"Would you personally vouch for both of them?"

"For Jensen, yes. I'd like to know more about Ellen. And I'll qualify my vote for Jensen by saying that I'll vouch for him as much as you can vouch for anyone these days. As far as his abilities go, I'd put my life in his hands in space."

"You'll be doing that if he's chosen," J.J. said. "Anyone aboard could abort the project or destroy it completely. You know how many ways there are aboard ship to do damage."

Dom nodded. "Still, you have to have crew."

"Have you had a briefing lately on the world situation?" He continued without waiting for an answer. "The Worldsavers are in complete control in China. They're training an army. Japan is pulling out of space to avoid invasion from China. The government fell in the U.K. and the new prime minister has put both Worldsavers and Earthfirsters in his cabinet. France is tottering. Germany is going through the throes of repression of individual rights in an effort to wipe out the Firsters there. It's civil war for all practical purposes. The Russians are compromising with their own Firsters. They've pulled five exploration ships out of space and are refitting them to carry phosphates."

"And here?" Dom asked.

"It's strangely quiet," J.J. said. "There hasn't been a major incident in months, not since the battle of DO-SEWEX. It's as if they're mustering their strength. There's the usual claptrap in the media and in Congress, but the killers are being quiet. A lot of people, including the FBI, are worried. Hedges reports to me from over there that several FBI plants have been exposed and killed in the last month. He thinks he has a top-level traitor right in the Washington office, and he's working desperately to find out what's going on. His private theory is that there'll be one major push before we can take off for Jupiter."

"Any guesses as to what kind of push?"

"Maybe revolution," J.J. said.

"It's that bad?"

"Take one small unit," J.J. said, "that squad of space marines at DOSEWEX. It was fifty percent infiltrated. How many Firsters are in a company of the army? A dozen men could wipe out a company if they hit a barracks in the middle of the night, killing men who thought they were buddies."

"You think armed revolution would succeed?"

"I don't know. No one does, because we don't know their strength. There are times when I feel that ninety percent of the population must be radical or radical in sympathy, but the great and unwashed masses are still a question mark. Would they support a radical armed revolution? In spite of what's been done to democracy in the name of equality of opportunity and freedom from want, there just might be a strong, hard core of democracy in the masses. It's impossible to guess how the public would turn. They hear political promises day after day, and day after day their food gets worse. They might buy the Firsters' propaganda. Get the world out of space and the milk and honey will flow."

"But, damnit, phosphates from Mars fertilize the fields which feed them," Dom said.

"We know that. Tell it to a welfare bum in Detroit who wants real steak every day instead of once a month. The Firsters tell him they'll develop better agricultural methods with the money now wasted in space."

"Is anyone thinking of a preemptive strike against them?" Dom asked.

"We think about it, but they're spread all over the country. They mass only for specific attacks, such as on DOSEWEX. They have no strong, individual leaders. They're splintered. That't the thing which has saved us so far. There's almost as much blood shed in fighting between radical groups jockeying for power as in their attacks on the government. If they ever form a united front, it will be big trouble, and that's one thing they might be doing now. If they were having internal consolidation meetings, that would account for the quiet."

"I've got a flight to catch," Dom said.

"There's time," J.J. said, looking at his watch. "Dom, when you get back, I want you to take charge of the security forces on the moon. Start a system of rotating teams, the membership changing each day at random. If they're planning something there it might help break up their organization."

"Will do."

J.J. looked thoughtful. "You know, if we could just feed the world we'd break the radicals in five years. There's a certain strength in what has often been called the average man. All he wants to do is live a peaceful and good life with enough food on the table to feed his family, good programs on the tube, a few luxuries. You know when this mess really started? It started when the shortage of petroleum took the citizen's automobile away from him. That is the dominant factor in our current troubles. The automobile gave a man freedom. When he was at the wheel of his own vehicle, he could feel that he was in control of his own fate. He had freedom of movement. In his car, he was isolated from the world, freed of his worries. That's when the discontent began, when the oil ran out. That left room for the nuts, the people who have such overwhelming egos that they think they're more capable of running things than anyone else. They don't care how many people starve, how many are killed. They just want to give orders. They want to instill fear in others. We've had them on Earth since the earliest recorded history, since Sargon the Conqueror, of old Ur. The power types. A kid reads two books and thinks he knows how to run the world. The idealists, the nuts, the sadists, the out-and-out psychos. They're joined by shiftless malcontents who are interested only in loot and plunder. If we could feed the world there'd be support against them. We could use the common decency of mankind to overcome the Sargon complex and then man would be unstoppable."

Dom arrived on the moon hours after two Earth-firsters died in a soundless explosion while trying to smuggle explosives into the shuttle area. He put J.J.'s orders into effect. Things were quiet for days. *Kennedy* was nearing completion.

The big boom came on a Sunday morning. It came in the form of a small freighter which had been Earthside for repairs. The incident demonstrated the most frightening penetration to date, for the small nuclear bomb aboard the freighter must have been placed there at Canaveral base.

The ship approached the lunar base on schedule, in contact with control, and veered off at the last minute to accelerate into a suicidal collision course with the *Kennedy* as she orbited, huge and vulnerable. A missile from the surface got the freighter while she was still far enough away so that the explosion did no damage to *Kennedy*. The flash lit the surface of the moon and blinded a few workers who happened to be watching the freighter.

The near miss inspired Dom. He knew that it was going to give J.J. a bad moment, for he did not want to risk compromising his plan through communications which could be intercepted. He stopped all flights from the moon to Earth and sent down the news that radical terrorists had destroyed an experimental ship, the *John F. Kennedy*. The news was greeted with public cheers and private gloom on Earth, and it brought J.J. on the next ship. He looked ten years older.

"How bad is it?" he asked, when Dom met him at the landing pad.

"J.J., I hated to do it to you," Dom said. "She's all right and untouched."

J.J. used choice parts of a vocabulary built from years of service and, having let off steam, took a drink and whooped in relief. He had to admit that it was a good idea. Now there would be no further attempts on the *Kennedy* from Earthside and they merely had to control the underground members on the moon. He

delayed sending down a one-man courier ship to give
the correct story to top DOSE brass.

No calls were allowed to go out to Earth. Travel was
frozen. Marine guards stood watch over all communications facilities, their individual members shifted in
random patterns.

A ship carrying the two remaining crew members
was allowed to land. Dom's first choices had checked
out. The engineer, Paul Jensen, was short, dark, a
silent man in his fifties. Ellen Overman, life-systems
specialist, was in her thirties, a tiny woman, small in
every respect, but perfectly proportioned, dark-haired,
brown eyes, a beautiful woman; she was talkative and
thrilled at being a part of the project.

J.J. sent down word that the Firsters had destroyed
the moon's water supplies, built up over a period of
many years and constantly recycled. A fleet of tankers
began to arrive, supposedly to replenish the moon's
water supply, but actually to fill the *Kennedy's* hold with
water. It was against all common sense to take an untested ship into space with a full cargo, but as Dom
continued to point out, she would work or she
wouldn't, and if she couldn't carry a load of water she
couldn't go down into Jupiter's atmosphere. The water
would be a valuable bonus in the operation. Taking it
to Mars would add only a few days to the trip, since
the planets were in the proper configuration, and it
would be a boon to dry Mars. The *Kennedy's* cargo
would represent a year's supply of water for the planet.

Neil Walters pronounced the *Kennedy* as ready as
she'd ever be without extensive in-flight testing. He,
too, disliked carrying a full cargo, but he shrugged and
said, "What the hell?" If she could fly at all the weight
of the water was insignificant. She had enough power
to lift a hundred times the weight without strain. If she
failed, it would not be for lack of power.

J.J. called a briefing in his quarters. He was in field uniform. He had two comets on his collar.

Dom saw the new insignia. "Congratulations, admiral."

"Just a belated recognition of ability, Flash," J.J. said. "When we bring home the bacon I'm going to see to it that you get one of these little doodads." He tapped a comet insignia.

"You're all heart," Dom said, remembering that it was J.J. who had refused his last chance at promotion because he'd happened to take a swing at a stupid and inefficient one-comet admiral.

"Meantime, you're promoted to captain," J.J. said. "You deserve it and the *Kennedy* deserves it. I wouldn't want her to be commanded by a mere commander."

The others arrived one by one. J.J. went through the chain of command aboard ship, although all were familiar with it already. Dom was in overall command. Neil was flying captain. J.J. was third in command, second to Neil in flying matters, to Dom in matters of ship's operation and safety. When the briefing was completed, J.J. made a little speech. He concluded by saying that things looked good.

"We'll announce the truth when we're in space," he said. "Right now the rads think their lousy suicides blew up the *Kennedy*. We've announced major cutbacks in the space program to give them another victory and, we hope, keep them quiet until we get back. We turned a billion and a half dollars back into the general fund. That made a big splash."

"So we're burning our bridges behind us," Doris said.

"Exactly," J.J. said grimly. "We bring home the bacon or we forget the space program. If we come back without it we'll be cut down to the Mars fertilizer run, and that won't last long before we'll be forced to pull all the ships home and close down the Mars base. But it had to be done. We think they were on the verge of armed revolt, and we weren't sure we could win. Now we've poured some oil on the troubled waters. They'll think they have unlimited time now. And we'll come back with something which will knock them on their asses and have the whole world on our side."

"I wish I could be as confident as you," Dom said.

"I have to be confident, Flash," J.J. said. "If I didn't feel that way I'd strap on as much plastique as I could carry and walk into an Earthfirster rally and pull the pin."

o 8 o

A million and one things can go wrong with a collection of complicated components, and the *Kennedy* was the most complex ship ever constructed. Every system aboard had been tested time and time again, but never in flight with all of them operating to move a huge mass of metal and a cargo of water.

Just in case, the entire backside of the moon was evacuated. Dom said a silent prayer, and he was sure that each of the others aboard were doing the same as Neil, buckled into the pilot's chair, finished the last preflight checklist and looked over at J.J. and winked. Neil's blue eyes were squinted and his mouth twisted into a grin which was not amusement, but his way of showing tension.

There was no dramatic countdown. When all systems were ready and all the thousands of little things checked out, J.J. gave a thumbs-up sign and Neil pressed a switch which ignited the preheater. Down in the engineroom Paul Jensen saw the light go on and ran a visual of the automatics. The sound of the preheater was a muffled rumble in Jensen's ears. There was a tiny vibration which only a trained man would notice. It came up to his senses through the soles of his feet.

"All right, baby," Neil said. "Do it for old Neil."

When the awesome power began to build there was

no loud noise, only a small hum. The sensation of power was there, however, and something in the closed atmosphere of the ship seemed to absorb it, to become alive with it. There was a charge in the air, a tingling which went beyond skin-deep to become a part of the entire sensory system.

Slowly power overcame inertia. Slowly the heavily laden monster of a ship moved, the force which powers the stars building, building, as crew members checked and reported, and it was "Go. Go. Go."

Dom's eyes flashed back and forth among an array of instruments which read stress and loading on hull and internal components. Inertial strain registered and was noted, but she had been built well, built with pride and loving care by men who felt that she might be the last of her breed, the last ship they'd ever build.

Acceleration was smooth and more rapid than a conventional rocket. The moon's gravity was a mere feather of force to be brushed aside by the brute power in *Kennedy's* drive.

Up and out she went smoothly. Neil goosed her, and the sudden acceleration pushed the crew against the backs of their seats. She was in position to turn, to assume the stance for the long, hard drive for acceleration which would take her to a rendezvous with Mars. She did it with only a fraction of her available muscle, a creature of free space, proud, beautiful, huge. There she lay as the crew examined her from stem to stern.

Although she handled like a dream and was doing great, Neil Walters was still aware that he was flying an untested ship with a crew aboard. He knew that *Kennedy* had been a crash project, and he didn't like flying the results of crash projects. He knew his space history. The first crash construction project produced the Vanguard series of rockets, and he'd seen the old films of Vanguards melting down on the launch pad. Crash programs did that. In the 1950s, the United States had pushed hard to catch up with the Russians, who had put a dog, Laika, into space with a total payload of over one thousand pounds. Up to that point the prestige of the United States had rested on a super job of jury-rigging by a crew under Wernher von Braun. They used spit and scrap wire, antique rockets, a lot of determination and imagination, and placed thirty-point-eight pounds of payload into orbit with a tiny Jupiter C.

Von Braun proved that crash techniques do not always fail, but still there was the Vanguard, which blew with spectacular regularity to prove that if you persist in crash techniques in things as complicated as space hardware you're going to have a few loud bangs.

The big question in Neil's mind was this: Was the *Kennedy* an inspired job of jury-rigging in the von Braun mold, or was she a Vanguard? If she stayed in one piece and performed, future historians would call her a technical miracle. If she blew, or simply fizzled, brought down by the failure of one tiny and relatively insignificant system somewhere deep inside her, they would go back to calling her what she was called in the beginning, *Folly*.

She checked out. Doris' computer ticked out, for the automatics, course settings and power settings and thousands of pieces of individual information which formed the word "Go."

Neil missed the familiar bellow of burning rockets, soundless in space, loud and all-pervasive inside a ship. His eyes squinted again as he activated her and started her on that long, long drive. His voice was professionally calm. His words went to the crew and on a tight beam back to Lunar Control.

"All systems normal, all systems go."

The next pucker period began, an attempt to get the

big bird up to cruising speed without blowing her wide open. It was more than just opening a throttle, but it was handled, in its complexity, by the shipboard computers, matching power to stress, every action monitored in a half-dozen ways, both electronic and visual. The ship hummed with that inaudible energy and began to move, faster and faster, the acceleration creating an artificial gravity pushing the crew members backward in their seats.

She didn't blow. Neil kept the crew working long hours during that initial period of acceleration. She reached cruise speed sixty-five percent faster than conventional ships and was moving faster than anything man had built. Every system was checked and rechecked, tested in flight.

At last Neil was satisfied. Rotating watches began, and some of the crew had time for a nap. The *Kennedy* performed as if she'd gone through the most thorough flight testing.

Neil took first watch. Dom, who had the second watch, knew he would be unable to sleep. He stayed near his panel, checking stress and loading. Paul Jensen kept an eye on the powerplant. Only Doris and Art retired to their cabins.

It was J.J. who took the call from Lunar Base. Even before the message was complete, his hand flicked an alarm and the lights flashed and the alarm whooped throughout the ship.

With the crew at emergency quarters, J.J. fed the message from the base into the sound system.

"*John F. Kennedy,* this is Moon Control."

"Moon Control, this is *J.F.K.*"

"*J.F.K.,* Admiral Pinkerton speaking. Please alert your crew. We have received a bomb threat. Repeat, there is a bomb threat directed against the *Kennedy.*"

"I am now going live to Moon Control," J.J. said. "Moon Control, this is *Kennedy*. Details, please."

"*J.F.K.*, a team of Earthfirsters have seized control station eight-five with its communications intact. We estimate the number of terrorists at five. We are in contact with them. They have made two demands. One, the *Kennedy* returns moonside. Two, we broadcast, and I quote, 'our guilt,' unquote, to the world."

J.J. shook his head impatiently. "Details on bomb threat, please."

"Stand by, *J.F.K.* The following is a recording of our communications with the terrorist in control of station eight-five."

There was a click and then an excited young voice. "Moon Control, Moon Control, this is the voice of freedom. Listen carefully. We are in control of station eight-five. We are heavily armed. We can resist any attack. Listen carefully. The folly of imperialism, the spaceship you call the *John F. Kennedy,* will be destroyed unless you meet the following requirements. One, you will order the *Kennedy* to return to Moon Base immediately. Two, you will broadcast to the world an abject apology for your wastefulness in allowing such a crime to be perpetrated on the people of the Earth, for using materials and money which should have gone to feed our starving millions. Three, you will provide a ship of the Explorer class to transport this group of freedom fighters to a free port Earthside."

The voice of Admiral Pinkerton was back. "We had them repeat it. He repeated it word for word as if he were reading."

"Moon Control, did you ask for details about a possible bomb on board the *Kennedy*?"

"That is affirmative. They merely read the message again."

Dom cut into the communications. "Admiral, this is

Dominic Gordon. Can you patch me into direct contact with the terrorists?"

"That is affirmative, Captain Gordon. In fact, they have the facilities to monitor this channel in station eight-five."

Dom tended to forget his new rank.

"I want to speak with them direct, admiral," he said.

"Hold one. You will be notified when we've established contact."

As Dom waited, the others were already in action. The *Kennedy* was the most instrumented ship ever built, and it was possible to check every inch of her with instruments. Signals were sent. Servos probed and measured. Every gram of material aboard the ship was recorded carefully in Doris' computer. She worked rapidly. She had the computer check everything aboard, clothing, personal effect, supplies. Every gram aboard was recorded, and two checks did not find even a tiny additional amount of mass. The check was complete before the radio patch was made.

"Dom," Doris said. "There's nothing aboard this ship we don't know about."

"Unless it was integrated into a structural piece during construction," Dom said. "Then it would show as a portion of the original mass."

"My guess is that they're bluffing," J.J. said.

"It's a good possibility, but can we gamble on it?" Dom asked.

"If we give in and take her back, she'll never leave the moon again. If we make that broadcast to the world it will have the same effect as blowing her up in space," J.J. said.

"With a small difference," Neil said. "If we take her back we'll be alive."

"Do you think you'd enjoy life as a groundling, Neil?" J.J. asked.

"You've got a point," Neil said.

"Jensen," Dom said into the communications system, "I want you to go over the engineroom with everything you've got, including your fingertips. The rest of us will use portable sniffers. Tune the sniffers to plastique. That's the material most used by the Firsters. Ellen, you take the food supplies. If there's a bomb aboard, my best guess is in supplies. If it was built into the ship, then I'd say they'd aim for the engineroom, where it would do the most damage. Doris, run me this problem. Give me a reading on what it would take to make it seem that the *Kennedy* is decelerating and then turning back to the moon. They might be measuring the strength of our radio transmissions. We want them to think we're following their orders, at least for a while. Unless they carried it in with them, and it's unlikely, they don't have visual equipment in station eight-five."

It took Doris three minutes. "I've set up an automatic power curve into the radio. The signals will grow slightly weaker at a decelerating ratio and then grow stronger."

"*J.F.K.*, this is Moon Control. Ready on your radio patch. Go ahead station eight-five."

"Gordon," said the young and tense voice, "this is the voice of freedom."

"The voice of a punk, you mean," Dom said. "I want you to listen and listen carefully. We're calling your bluff. We've checked every atom of weight aboard this ship, and you're lying. There is no bomb aboard. We're heading out and we'll continue to accelerate. I just wanted the personal satisfaction of telling you, because in about one minute I'm going to order Moon Security to blast station eight-five with one small newk. Burn happily, punk."

He waited, eyes troubled.

The young voice seemed to be just short of hysteria.

"You're the punk, Gordon. You're the one who is robbing the people. You're the one who's going to die, you and all the other parasites aboard. We can detonate the bomb from here, or if you use your newk on us it will go off with its own timer. Either way you're dead. This is your last chance to turn back. You'll be given a fair trial before a tribunal of the people."

"Punk," Dom said, "you have about one minute to live. You don't seem to understand that we're wise to you. You're all mouth. There's no way you punks could get a bomb aboard. No way. Goodbye, punk. Moon Control, this is Captain Gordon. I order that in exactly one minute you send one small nuclear warhead right down the gut of station eight-five. *J.F.K.* over and out."

The next voice was different, low, smooth, unexcited. "Good try, Captain Gordon," the man's voice said. "We who love freedom don't believe in needless shedding of blood, nor in the waste of resources. If we did, I would push the button myself. However, we would like to salvage the *Kennedy* for scrap to build factories for production of consumer goods for the people."

"Anyone recognize the voice?" Dom asked, over the intership circuits.

"I assure you, Captain Gordon, that there is a bomb and that it will go off at a time of our choosing. I can guarantee that the *Kennedy* will be destroyed totally. I can promise you that she'll burst open like a melon and that all of you will die with her."

"I've got him," Art said into Dom's earphones. "He's service, in charge of loading the water. His name is Bensen."

"The damned water," Dom said, throwing aside the phones. "It's in the damned water. He said we'd burst open like a melon. One small charge wouldn't burst this ship open unless the force were compressed by a large volume of water. Let's go."

"Captain Gordon?" the smooth, calm voice said.

Dom went back to the radio. "Go ahead."

"I am pleased to note that in spite of your brave talk you are presently decelerating."

"You have radio scanners, then," Dom said.

"We do. We estimate full stop and turnaround at 2130 Zulu."

"Hold one," Dom said. Then, leaving the communicator open, "Please give me an estimate of turnaround time."

"2134 Zulu," Doris said.

"Station eight-five," Dom said, "turnaround time is 2134 Zulu."

"Noted," Bensen said. "And now Admiral Pinkerton will make his broadcast to Earth."

Dom said, "The broadcast will be made at 2134 Zulu, our turnaround time."

There was a silence. He could imagine the terrorists consulting among themselves, trying to figure out why he insisted on waiting two hours and forty minutes before making the broadcast. Evidently they decided that the delay could do their cause no harm, since the *Kennedy* was obeying orders.

"That is agreeable," Bensen said. "It will give us time to pass the text of the statement to be broadcast to the people of Earth to Moon Control."

"J.J., take communications," Dom said. He grinned. Hell, command was not so difficult after all. "Neil, it's you and me. We have two hours and thirty-nine minutes to find that bomb."

"I'm with you," Neil said.

Neil was into his suit before Dom. He had more practice. He checked Dom's life-support gear and turned to allow Dom to check his backpack. Less than five minutes had elapsed when they entered a lock chamber offering access to the hold, that vast space which made up the main volume of the ship and which was filled with thousands of tons of pure water from Earthside purification plants.

"Any idea where to start?" Dom asked, his internal suit radio on open channel to be broadcast throughout the ship.

"I have estimated that it would take a minimum of five kilos of plastique to blow her," Doris said. Her voice was cool, professional. "However, with the masses I'm dealing with in the hold I can't distinguish so small a weight. The problem is compounded by a minor difference in temperature in various hold sections, enough to vary weight per unit of water."

"Make a note of that," Dom said. "In future we'll want to be able to scan the interior of the hold. Right now we have to figure on combing every inch of the hold, right?"

"I'm afraid so," Doris said.

"Maximum effect would be obtained by placing the charge near the geometric center," Neil said.

"Good thinking," Dom said. "We'll start from the center bulkheads and work toward bow and stern. I'll go sternward, Neil. I'd say check the hogging girders and bulkhead supports first. Bensen must be sharp enough to realize that convection currents will be set up in this mass of water, so if he wanted to keep his blast near the center of mass, he'd secure it so that it wouldn't float around on the currents."

"That's a roger," Neil said.

The lock filled and opened into the hold. Dom could feel the psychological weight of tons of water on him as he moved out into the vastness. The blackness was total. Their lights made lances of brightness into the pit ahead of them. They swam side by side through huge bays of the hold and reached the center after what seemed to Dom to be miles of swimming. They were back to back for a moment, light beams pointing in different directions. Dom moved off, moving his head to direct the light. Reaching the first system of supports, he began a swift but careful search. He noted the time required to completely examine the bulkhead and did a calculation in his head. At that rate the bomb would explode, estimating that the terrorists would act when the turnaround time came and went and no broadcast went out to Earth, before they could cover half of the hold area.

He had never liked being underwater. He was a creature of the openness of space. He wanted space around him, the reach of interplanetary distance, not the oppressive weight of a liquid. He fought the urge to swim upward, although there was no up, to reach for the surface and for air. Even in the smallest ships he had never felt so confined as he did by the dark weight of the water in the hold. He forced himself to breathe evenly, for he tended to pant. He swam onward toward the next set of girders.

"I spent too much time at that first bulkhead," he said.

"Roger," Neil answered. "And ditto."

"And if we just hit the most likely places we could miss the mother," Dom said. "There's no choice. We just have to search carefully and hope that he put it near the center so that we'll find it before turnaround time."

"Captain Gordon," Ellen Overman said, "I am qualified for life-support-system work."

"Do you remember from your indoctrination how the internal supports are constructed?" Dom asked.

"Roger," Ellen said.

"Suit up, then," Dom said. "Come in through lock

four and move toward the bow. If you see anything
don't try to handle it yourself."

"I am also qualified to handle explosives," Ellen
said.

"Dom," Art said, "I can suit up, too."

"Not a chance," Dom said. "Not with your lungs."

"I can handle it," Art said.

"Stay where you are, and that's an order," Dom
said.

"You've been down fifteen minutes," Doris said.
"Two hours and twenty-four minutes to turnaround."

"They might give us a few extra minutes," Dom
said.

"Don't count on it," J.J. said. "We'd better figure
them to panic when we don't start that broadcast on
time. By that time that bomb had better be in free
space a long way from the hull. If Bensen and his nuts
get the idea we're trying to be tricky they'll push the
button without a moment's hesitation."

"I can't figure why they want the *Kennedy* to return
to the moon anyhow," Paul Jensen said. "It would be
to their advantage to blow her up in space. Then they
could be sure she'd never fly again."

"That's the way I had it figured," Dom said, "when
I told them we wouldn't broadcast until we were
turned. I figured they'd blow the bomb the minute the
broadcast was over. I just didn't want to worry anyone
with my private fears."

"You two are little rays of sunshine," Neil said.

Dom was swimming around and through a maze of
hogging girders. His light picked up dozens of little
angles which would offer excellent spots to plant a
bomb.

"I think we can figure it that way," J.J. said. "The
minute the broadcast is finished, they bust the button."

"My God," Ellen Overman said, as she emerged from the lock into the hold. "It's big."

"There are no sharks," Dom said. "That's in our favor. Move forward. You'll make visual contact with a girder system."

"Got it," Ellen said, "Don't worry about me. I just felt lonely there for a second."

"Twenty-five minutes," Doris said.

The pattern was set and would continue with mounting tension for the next two hours. Doris called out the time used at five-minute intervals, and Dom began to match his movements to five-minute units.

By turnaround time just over half of the hull supports would have been examined.

At the end of the first hour Dom began to fear that he had bet the lives of his crew and the existence of the ship on a snap judgment that the terrorists would have tried for maximum force by placing the charge near the center of mass. Doubts made him sweat inside his suit, and the fluid reclamation system had to work hard. He and Neil continued to work away from each other, moving away from the center. Ellen was forward, working in the same direction as Neil. At the end of one and a half hours, Neil reached bulkhead seven-three, where Ellen had begun her search. He resisted an urge to check behind her. If she missed it, she missed it. It was all a guessing game anyhow. There was always the chance that the charge was not even in the hold, but elsewhere in the ship. He swam rapidly and caught up to Ellen within a few minutes.

"Nice to have company," she said.

"We'll try it together and see if we get in each other's way," Neil said. "You go port on the next bulkhead."

They moved faster than Dom, who was still working alone. J.J. announced the passage of one hour and fifteen minutes. The huge central area of the ship seemed endlessly long.

"I have a very interesting phenomenon," Doris said. "Your movements send energy impulses against the hull. I got faint readings when all of you were swimming alone, and now with Neil and Ellen close together the force generated by their movements is strong enough to register well."

"So?" Dom asked.

"Nothing, really," Doris said. "But based on the readings I'd say that the hull could take an explosion of just under one and a half kilos of Dupont XP without rupture."

"That might be encouraging if we knew that the explosive is merely Dupont XP and not more than one and a half kilos," J.J. said.

"They had the new German stuff in the Gulfport raid last month," Art said. "It's twenty-five percent more potent."

"Yeah, leave it to the Germans," Dom said.

"Dupont XP is the standard explosive used on the moon," Doris said.

"Let's not clutch at straws," Dom said. "I think our only chance is to find the charge and get it off the ship."

"What if time runs out?" J.J. asked.

"Evacuate the ship," Dom said. "J.J. and Doris in capsule one. Art and Ellen in the pilot's capsule with Neil. I'll go with Paul in the stern capsule, but I'm going to ask you to be prepared to stay longer than the others, Paul, to give me all the possible time down here."

"Allowing two minutes for emergency capsule launch and enough time to allow the capsule to clear, you'll have to start out the locks no later than fifteen minutes to zero," Doris said.

"I can pop out the stern lock," Dom said. "We'll be launching away from the direction of thrust, so we'll cover distance faster with the ship pulling away. I can take an extra five minutes."

"That's cutting it too close," Doris said.

"No heroes on this trip, Flash," J.J. said. "I want you in that capsule at no less than zero minus twelve minutes."

"Roger," Dom said.

"We'll start a countdown at zero minus forty," J.J. said. "At zero minus fifteen, all aboard the capsule except Dom and Paul. At zero minus twelve, Dom and Paul board and launch. We rendezvous in the capsules on my signal on band seven-oh-three."

"This may be a stupid question," Paul said, "but how about opening the hold and letting the water out into space? We could search it in a fraction of the time."

"Good thinking," Dom said. "But if we vented through all loading hatches it would take five and a half hours."

"Sorry," Jensen said. "I'll stick to the powerplant."

"As a matter of fact, Paul," Dom said. "I want you to leave the powerplant now and run a visual and manual on the compartment bulkheads. If we have to abandon ship there's a chance she'll survive a small explosion. Be sure they're all closed."

"They read fine," Doris said.

"I'll feel better if they're checked," Dom said, swimming as rapidly as possible toward another bulkhead grouping.

"On my way," Jensen said.

"Dom, you've used one hour and thirty-nine minutes," Doris said. "Sixty minutes and counting."

"Captain Gordon," Jensen said, his voice grim, "are you a practicing psychic?"

"Only a practicing pessimist," Dom said. "Give it to me."

"The hatch locks on the redundant bulkheads are inoperative," Jensen said. "And the mains would have to take up any strain alone."

"The damned things were working when we checked them," Neil said.

"They're not working now," Jensen said.

The redundant bulkheads were safety features. Between the hold and the compartments forward and aft were two sets of bulkheads. The inner wall had no hatches or locks. The outer, or redundant, bulkhead was hatched, allowing access to the air space between bulkheads.

"All readings are normal," Doris said. "That clever little bit had to be built in."

"And something's happened since we checked," Neil said.

"A timed acid charge next to the wiring," J.J. said. "That would do it."

"That means we had Firsters working on the ship," Dom said. "It would take an instrumentation tech and an electrician working together to install acid vials and an inspector to overlook them."

"And how many more" J.J. asked, his voice seething with frustrated anger.

"Art, give Paul a hand and get cracking on those hatch controls," Dom said. "Get them closed and lock them."

All of the metal pieces which formed the internal supports had begun to look alike, giving Dom the fear that he had forgotten to move on and was pulling himself, swimming, using his hands for help, over the same girders time after time. He was getting very tired. When you're tired mistakes come more easily. He didn't want to overlook some small package, and he didn't want to have to slow down.

"Forward hatches closed and locked," Paul Jensen said. "Moving to the stern."

"Roger on that," Dom said.

Suddenly he was wishing for Larry. Larry could put himself inside the head of that sonofabitch back there on the moon and it was eighty to twenty that Larry could send searchers to within a hundred feet of the charge. Larry would think it over for a few minutes while telling bad jokes and then he'd say, "Hell, it's simple."

So try to put yourself in Larry's head, he told himself. Make it simple. What are the factors? A hint that the bomb was in the hold. Sabotaged hatch-closing controls on the safety bulkheads.

"Hell," he said aloud, "it is simple."

"What's so simple?" Neil asked.

"They had to plan this thing well in advance," Dom said, his voice showing his excitement. Even as he talked he was moving straight down the center of the hold, swimming for the stern bulkhead. "They wanted an explosion and they wanted it to do maximum damage. So they fixed it so that the safety hatches wouldn't close, so that the explosion, if it didn't rupture the outer hull, would do maximum internal damage. They want water in the forward quarters and in the engineroom."

"Sounds logical," J.J. said.

"Neil, you and Ellen stop where you are and swim like hell to the forward bulkhead."

"Forty and counting, Flash," J.J. said. "Are you ready to bet it all on a hunch?"

"That is affirmative," Dom said. "We'll find it on the stern bulkhead or near it. Just in case they got two charges, I want Neil and Ellen to cover the forward bulkhead. My bet is that they're aiming at the engine compartment."

He pictured it. The main bulkhead ruptured, water pouring into the engine compartment through the open safety hatches. It wouldn't even have to be a huge charge. A small shaped charge would punch a hole in the bulkhead.

Neil said, "We're moving. I think you're right, Dom. A three-foot hole punched in the bulkhead would do it."

"Probably near a seam," Doris said.

Dom was gasping. The beam of his light sliced the water ahead. The minutes seemed to race by. When he could see the distinctive contours of the stern bulkhead he slowed and allowed his heart to catch up, gliding forward on inertial momentum. The bulkhead was studded with diamond-shaped reinforcement for strength. He came onto it at the approximate center. It extended up and down and out on all sides, a large area of potential hiding places, and each reinforcement diamond offered multiple planes for planting a charge.

"We're under way up here," Neil said. "Ellen, go to the outer hull and start clockwise. Next to the outer hull would be a good place."

"Thirty-one and counting," Doris said.

"Paul and Art," Dom said, "when we find this mother we'll bring it out the nearest lock, so stand by to get there fast. Paul on lock controls, Art on the nearest outer lock. Everybody in life-support gear now. When we come out, I'll want a section closed off so that Art can have the outer lock already open. Got that?"

"Roger," Art said.

"Abandon-ship stations in fifteen minutes," J.J. said.

"Thirty and counting," Doris reported.

Never had minutes seemed to pass so quickly. Dom

was moving rapidly over the bulkhead, checking each depression between reinforcing diamonds, running his hands over the reinforcements themselves. Neil and Ellen reported no find.

The charge on the stern bulkhead was mounted a few inches from the outer hull on a flat surface between two reinforcement diamonds. It filled the space neatly. It was held in place by four gleaming nuts on studs into the bulkhead, itself.

"Neil," Dom said, "concentrate on the second row of depressions at six o'clock. I've got mine."

"Roger," Neil said.

"Twenty and counting," Doris said.

"Nothing here," Neil said.

"Take five more minutes, spend it down low," Dom said. "Paul, I need a half-inch power spanner and a two-foot repair limpet at the port stern lock. Start the lock cycling now. I'm betting that this thing is rigged to detonate if it's removed underwater." He waited near the inner lock door. "They went to too much trouble not to booby-trap it."

"The lock is flooded and opening," Paul said.

"We're negative up here," Neil reported.

"Roger," Dom said. "You and Ellen get out." Dom grabbed the repair limpet and the power wrench as the lock door opened.

"Sixteen and counting, Dom," Doris said.

"No change in orders," Dom said, as he swam back toward the charge. "Take abandon-ship stations."

"Change of orders," J.J. said. "I'm staying aboard. We'll get it off in time, Flash."

"This is a matter of safety," Dom said. "You're going off, admiral."

"Aye, aye, sir," J.J. said bitterly.

Dom was inflating the repair limpet, pumping water from around the charge. When it was enclosed inside the limpet he inserted his hands and carefully used the in-place cloths to dry the charge and bulkhead around it. He inserted the spanner, activated it, spun off one of the nuts.

"Fifteen and counting," Doris said. "Capsules ready for launching."

Two nuts were off. A third was coming.

"Number one launched," Doris said.

"Pilot's capsule launched," Neil said. "We'll expect to be back aboard in a few minutes, Dom."

"That's a hopeful roger," Dom said, spinning off the last stud and removing the spanner.

"Standing by," Paul Jensen said. "It's just you and me, Dom."

He allowed the capsules forty-five seconds to clear the ship, at least by a few hundred feet. Then he pulled on the charge. It came and his heart thumped as he waited for it to blow. It stuck. He used the spanner as a pry and it came off the studs and was in his hand inside the repair limpet. He turned it. It was rigged to explode upon contact with water. He closed a watertight bag over the charge and removed it from the limpet, letting the limpet fall away.

"Stand by to operate the lock, Paul," he said. He swam into the lock and the door started closing behind him. The explosive device was sophisticated. It was equipped for detonation by radio signal, and it was standard to have the circuits rigged to explode if there was tampering.

"Four minutes and counting," Doris said.

"I'm in the lock and I have the charge," Dom said. But he knew as well as they that it took five minutes to empty the lock and another few seconds to open the outer door, run down the airless corridor and send the charge into space.

"Dom," J.J. said. "Moon Control is on. They have

been warned that if the broadcast does not start exactly on time the charge will be detonated."

"J.J., goddammit, you're supposed to be off the ship."

"Put me on report," J.J. said. "You'll make it."

"Stall them. Tell them to stall somehow. All we need is another couple of minutes," Dom said. The water was being pumped out of the lock with a terrifying slowness. The heavy charge in his hands seemed so inert, but it was death, not only for him but for the ship.

"Three minutes, Flash. Moon Control says stalling is out. They've been warned against it."

"All right," Dom said. "Tell them to start the broadcast on time. It should last a couple of minutes, at least. That just might give us time."

The water was only down a couple of feet from the ceiling on the lock. Seconds ticked off his wrist chronometer.

"Those miserable bastards," J.J. said. "Those mucking, murdering bastards. Dom, it has been decided at the top level that the service will not appease the terrorists. They will not start the broadcast. We have two minutes and—fifty seconds."

Dom was feeling panic, but his mind worked, envisioning the layout of the ship. The hold lock and the outer hull lock were almost opposite each other across the narrow walkway alongside the hold, nothing more than a tunnel connecting the forward compartments with the engine areas.

"Paul," Dom yelled. "Can you override the safeties on the hold lock?"

"Affirmative."

"Do it. Outer hull lock open?"

"I'm in vacuum. Affirmative."

"When I give the word, brace yourself in somewhere

and blow the door to this lock. Don't get in the way. A lot of water will be sucked out."

"I've got you," Jensen said. "Take a minute."

"You have just over that," J.J. said.

"Safety off," Jensen said. "Clumsy. It will take a little repair."

"We'll worry about that later," Dom said. "Blow this door as fast as you can, right now."

He placed himself against the door, the charge in its watertight bag held down toward the deck. When the door started up, the vacuum in the corridor and all the space would suck the water out of the lock with tremendous force.

"Here we go," Jensen said.

The door started upward. There was a roaring hiss as explosive decompression started in the lock, sucking water under the door opening so rapidly that Dom almost went with it, catching himself with one hand on a support as the force tore at him. The charge was ripped from his hand. It banged against the rising door and then shot out and then with the same suddenness with which it began decompression was complete and there was silence. Dom closed his eyes and waited for the explosion. The lock door continued to rise. He looked out into the tunnel and saw Jensen still clinging to supports. If there was another charge it would go about now.

He did not hear the explosion when it came, for it came in the vacuum of space fifty yards away and slightly astern of the open outer lock. The blast which would have been so deadly in the filled hold was puny in the emptiness of space. Later, an examination showed a few pinpoints of damage on the skin of the hull.

"Mr. Jensen," Dom said, very formally and very softly, "you may close hull."

He went forward to discover that each member of the crew was in his or her place, that the reported launchings of the escape capsules had been faked for his benefit. He was both angered by having his orders disobeyed and touched to know that each of them had risked his life to stay and do whatever was possible to save the ship.

"What can I say?" J.J. asked. " 'Good work' would be a feeble way to express it."

"You can have your say when I put you on report for ignoring a ship captain's order," Dom said.

He felt a sudden weakness in his knees and sat down. Doris handed him a cup of steaming coffee.

"I think I've created a monster," J.J. said. "Give a junior officer a bit of authority and it goes to his head."

"Save it," Dom said. "You'll need the energy. We're going to go over this ship. I don't want any more little surprises. I want every circuit, every component, every inch of her checked."

Doris was watching his face, a strange little smile on her lips.

"And you," he said. "I thought you were safe in the capsule."

"I'm sorry," she said. "I couldn't. There were several reasons."

"Dom," Neil said, "there was no way any of us were going to let this ship die and go back to the moon on a rescue vessel."

Dom was thinking about those several reasons Doris had for staying on the ship as long as he was there and in danger.

"All right," he said. "I suppose I'm supposed to be grateful. I am, personally, but as captain of this ship I want it to be known that this is the last mutiny. Understood?"

"Yes, sir," J.J. said, grinning.

"Admiral," Dom said. "Let's get started. You, sir, can start with the heads."

And even the heads were checked during the next few exhausting days before they were satisfied that the *Kennedy* held no more unpleasant surprises for them. The guess that the circuits to the hatches in the redundant bulkheads had been burned with a delayed acid bomb was correct. The damage was minor. Within hours after the explosion of the bomb in space the men who had seized station eight-five on the moon were dead. Meanwhile, as the check of the ship continued, Mars grew from a star to a small globe on the viewscreens, and the unimpressive red disc grew rapidly as the shipboard activities settled into a routine.

o 9 o

In deep space a ship becomes a small world. While
there is radio contact with the moon and with the more
powerful stations at Houston and DOSEWEX, that
contact is limited to official and functional communications. Radio messages from the *Kennedy* should have
been less limited than those of an ordinary ship, for the
Kennedy had as much computer power as either of the
two main control stations. But since anyone on Earth
with a powerful receiver could monitor ship channels,
the *Kennedy* was limited in the information she could
safely send.

Still when things settled down and the watches became long and boring, a favorite form of entertainment
was to listen to traffic between ships in space and the
home control stations.

To be in deep space was to be cut off from any accurate knowledge of affairs on Earth, for the daily
broadcasts to spacers were from government-controlled
stations. Much of the news content of such programs
was shameless puffs of current Publicrat policies, promises of the Utopia to come. There was no mention of
the attempt to destroy the *Kennedy* or of the death
of the terrorists on the moon.

In the early days, when a few brave men were the
focus of the attention of the world, nothing was too
good for spacemen. On the first Mars flights the hours
of boredom were partially dispelled by broadcasts on a

114

special channel, news, music, and even long chats with relatives and friends of the men who were riding the ship through a long, tedious flight. Now, in the name of economy, broadcasts were limited and consisted mostly of propaganda.

No one aboard the *Kennedy* bothered to listen to the government stations. The ship carried a sizable film library and good music tapes. Because power was unlimited, there was a decent library of real books, plus a larger one of microfilm. Still, one of the favorite forms of passing time was to listen to the cool, professional voices of spacers sending reports to Houston.

For essential communications, the *Kennedy* was equipped with a squirter, a device which compacted voice messages into a split-second burst of energy and beamed the messages down to DOSEWEX, where they were recorded, stretched, and decoded. Messages were received in the same way, and only J.J. had access to the decoder. He held briefings on important communications. He was concerned by a new, all-out attack on the space program. Budget cutting in Congress was only one symptom. There was nothing definite as yet, but the FBI reported an apparent lessening of competition among the various radical groups. One indication was an attack on the DOSE communications station during which both Earthfirsters and Worldsavers had been killed.

One of the persistent questions sent by J.J. asked who had made the decision, at the last minute, to reverse a continuing policy of appeasement in dealing with terrorists.

"It is very strange," he said, "because for years I've advocated a get-tough policy. I have always said that it would be best, in the long run, to sacrifice a few lives by refusing ransom demands. Sure, it would be rough on the victims, but it would save lives over the long period. For years I've been overruled from the political side. A gang of terrorists takes a hostage and demands the release of imprisoned terrorists, or money, or some political objective. In the past the bleeding hearts have forced us to give in in the name of saving the life of the hostage. Then, all of a sudden, when there's more at stake than there ever has been, when the *Kennedy* herself is the pawn, when the last hope for space is the prize, we embark on a new policy of non-negotiation."

"A political decision?" Dom suggested. "Because the politicians really wanted the *Kennedy* to be destroyed?"

"I've asked repeatedly," J.J. said. "I get no answers. My main question is this. How did the Earthsiders find out about the situation when the moon was blocked off from any communications?"

"Any one of a dozen facilities could have broken radio silence," Doris said.

"Or someone in Washington could have known in advance about Benson's bomb," J.J. said. "Someone at a high level had to be involved to get a bomb into Canaveral for that first attempt, and ditto to getting Bensen assigned to load the water."

"Admiral Pinkerton?" Neil asked.

"He has only a couple of years to go before retirement," J.J. said. "He's had a good career. I don't see him as a traitor to the service."

"That's the problem," Dom said. "Who can we trust? There had to be a relatively high-level traitor at DOSEWEX to arrange the raid there."

"We have one advantage," J.J. said. "We know we're fighting for survival, not only for the space program but for all of humanity. I seem always to be giving pep talks, but what the hell. It all boils down to seven people, us. We bring back the bacon or that's it for space. The *Kennedy* will make a few Mars runs and then she'll be scrapped. The Mars stations will be closed. Eventually even the moon will be closed and we'll all be down there breeding ourselves into starvation. What follows will make the Dark Ages seem like an era of enlightenment."

"It makes you wonder, doesn't it?" Jensen asked. "Sometimes I think what we need is a man on horseback, a real leader."

"A military takeover of the government?" J.J. asked sternly.

"What government?" Jensen snorted. "That bunch of idiots in Washington?"

"Are you saying that you feel democracy has outlived its usefulness?" J.J. asked.

"There never has been true democracy," Jensen said. "And certainly not in recent years. Not with terrorists depriving people of their right to live, their right to make their own decisions."

J.J. nodded grimly. "There have always been criminals among us, but when the cities grew too large to be governed properly the criminals were more free to act. Sensible citizens locked themselves in their apartments when they were deprived of the right to walk the streets in safety, and the early efforts to remedy the situation were one hundred eighty degrees off target. The bleeding-heart school of sociologists said that the criminal was merely a product of his environment, that he was to be pitied. Criminal penalties grew steadily less severe. A man can commit murder now and either walk free or serve no more than three years in a government detention home which is much like a country club. When the bleeding hearts finally pushed through anti-gun legislation and confiscated all firearms from lawful citizens, they left enough arms in the hands of criminal types to start a revolution. Then the terrorists gained a foothold in the twentieth century. At first there was no international condemnation, because certain groups of terrorists had the secret support of certain countries. The individual had no protection against violence. Government failed to live up to the obligation to protect the people. Sensible men refused to remember that since the beginning, force can only be countered by force. Man has always been a predator, merciless to his fellow men. And when the majority lets a minority composed of predators control policy and topple governments, it's all over."

"You're saying that most of us have become overcivilized," Doris said.

"Or soft-headed." J.J. sighed. "Sure, it's humane to feel pity for the unfortunate and to help when it is possible. It is damned well not possible to give to every individual in the world the luxuries which, in the past, were the rewards for achievers. Take one absurd example. There just isn't enough gold in existence to give every person on earth a gold ring. There isn't enough of several commodities to give every woman a washing machine, a dishwasher, a toaster, a television set. The world was not meant to support so many people. And I think there is an overall design in the basic reality that the world alone cannot provide the ideal life for eight billion people."

"The old argument for space," Ellen said. "It is man's destiny to go into space, since his small world can't satisfy his needs."

"I think man's place is in space," Neil said, "but I don't belive in some predestined force. I think the stars are just there and it's immaterial to the universe whether man reaches them or not."

"There are still those who think we're going to come face to face with God out there in space and be blinded," Art said.

"Let's get back to Paul's suggestion of a man on

horseback," Neil said. "Suppose a leader did arise. Suppose he built an organization which could take over the United States. If he had one goal and one goal only, and that was to restore law and order, what actions would he take, and how far would people like us back him?"

"I'd want to know that sooner or later we'd return to a form of democracy," Doris said.

"I'd grab a weapon and enlist in his force," Paul said.

"I'd try to become an intimate of his and have a say in things." J.J. laughed. "But then I've always thought that a benevolent dictatorship was the finest and most efficient form of government."

"As long as I'm the benevolent dictator," Dom said. "But I'd back the right man, I guess. I know that things look bad, but we're not finished, not yet. Like Doris, I'd want to return to being a republic, not a democracy. No heirs to the great man allowed, to give power time to corrupt."

"I can think of a dozen men who'd handle things better than the politicians," Paul said.

"The sad thing is that the revolution, if there is one, is being run by the wrong people," Dom said.

"Perhaps, if we finish our mission, there won't be a revolution," J.J. said. "What we'll bring back will be revolutionary, but for the better. But Neil asked a good question. How far would we be willing to go, how many personal freedoms would we be willing to put into storage, in order to restore a bit of sanity in the world? Would we send armed soldiers to break up Earthfirster rallies and kill hundreds?"

"Would it be a loss?" Paul asked.

"I'd send them with fire guns," Neil said.

"I would first give them a chance to disperse peacefully," Ellen said.

"Hell, exterminate them where you find them," Neil said.

"My husband met force with force," Doris said. "He died."

There was a moment of silence. "We're a fine, bloodthirsty crew," Dom said. "If I decide to start a revolution I'll recruit all of you."

"Would it be inhumane to kill the terrorists in order to have peace?" J.J. asked.

"You're being very persistent with that question, aren't you?" Ellen asked.

"I'm curious," J.J. said. "Is it wrong to put the welfare of the race ahead of temporary considerations of personal freedom? Would we be labeled monsters by history if we killed thousands in order to make life better for millions?"

"That question is too big for me," Dom said.

"Because it could come to that," J.J. said. "You may be forced to take sides, to fight. Space and future hope, or Earth in isolation and slow rot. The future or the present. A loaf of bread for each citizen before starvation or some starvation now and plenty later."

"I can hope for a loaf now and more loaves in the future," Dom said. "I can hope that that alien on Jupiter has a sublight drive and we pull him out and he shares his secrets with us. I can hope that we'll build a fleet of starships and start sending out colonists to grow good wheat so that every man does not want for bread."

"I can go with that," J.J. said. "But what if the bogie is not a sublight ship? What if it is merely an unmanned probe which has been traveling for centuries? Sure, a sublight drive would solve all our problems, provided that there are rich, uninhabited planets out there. But what would solve our short-term problems and give us an opportunity to develop our own starships?"

"That's simple," Ellen said. "Food."

"Food," J.J. said. "All our recent efforts have been directed toward providing more food. We're going to Jupiter to try to salvage an alien ship in the hope that it will enable us to move the race to a new food supply. Food is the key. The man, or group of men, who provide the world with food can control the world without armed revolution. Do you agree?"

"Meaning that if we, as you say, bring home the bacon, the service will have a strong voice in policy?" Doris asked.

"Shouldn't we?" J.J. countered.

"So we're going to Jupiter so that we can tell other men what to do?" Doris asked.

"Hell, no," J.J. said. "We're going to Jupiter to get a few loaves of bread." He spread his hands. "But when it comes down to it, who would you rather have running things, service people or men like the senator from New Mexico?"

"Knowing some high-ranking service people, that's not much of a choice," Dom said.

"Flash, you wound me," J.J. said. He smiled. "There's been a method behind my madness in this discussion. I mentioned the gentleman from New Mexico. As of this morning, Pacific time, he announced that he has been the controlling force behind the Earthfirster movement. Further, he said that he has effected a union of all radical forces, with the two main groups being Firsters and Worldsavers, and that he intends to take over sole control of the government, either by peaceful means or by armed force."

"My God," Doris said.

Dom felt a cold chill run up his spine.

"There will be civil war," J.J. said. "When we return, we'll have to take sides."

"If it isn't over when we get back," Neil said.

"Who the hell will fight them?" Art asked. "Not the government in Washington."

"The Department of Space Exploration has joined with all branches of the service to declare loyalty to the government," J.J. said.

"The government is riddled with Firsters and Worldsavers," Dom said.

"The radicals walked out of Congress, declaring it an instrument of totalitarianism. There's no one left in Washington but the President, a few members of his cabinet, and a few very brave liberals."

"What a choice," Neil said. "The terrorists or the bleeding hearts."

"It's the only choice we have," J.J. said, "but you can easily see that if we muster enough force to beat them, we'll be running things when it's over. I mean the combined services."

"Has fighting actually started?" Ellen asked.

"It's fairly unorganized, for the moment." J.J. sighed. "There is a main force of radicals pushing eastward from California, picking up recruits as they move. Their target is probably DOSEWEX. A couple of the southern bases, one army and one naval base, have been taken. But mainly the losses have been in the northeast. The southern army and sea marine bases are furnishing most of the loyal troops. There's a defense line being drawn up running roughly from Chicago to the Texas gulf coast."

"Can it be held?" Neil asked.

"That remains to be seen. As it looks now, the services, with the exception of the space arms, which have a higher percentage of loyalty, seem to be divided about fifty-fifty."

"We could newk the bastards and get it over," Paul said.

"And poison our own country," J.J. said.

"Leave it so battered that the overseas radicals could walk in," Neil said.

"Right now we're fighting a limited war," J.J. said. "It's tough to slaughter your own people. You don't use nuclear weapons on your own country. You try to hold the damage down and pray that old John Q. Public will come up right, as he so often does. The unwashed masses. Sooner or later they're going to pull their heads out of their TV sets and realize that someone is shooting at them. The way John Q. moves will decide it. Right now there are two relatively small armies shooting at each other."

"The public will decide the issue on very intelligent thought," Paul said. "Like which side has the most photogenic generals and the prettiest uniforms."

"Maybe, maybe not," J.J. said. "One of the first results of the war will be the destruction of the distribution system. People will be scavenging for edible weeds in the fields. When that happens, we'll get right down to the nitty-gritty. If we can convince the public that hunger is the result of a war started by the radicals, they might come in on our side. Our mission takes on a new importance. Because if we can go back and promise them the stars—"

"And once we're in control give them the stars," Neil said.

Dom was numb. He kept hearing that phrase in his mind. Once we're in control. It was almost as if—but it was Doris who voiced his suspicions.

"J.J., you knew it was coming, didn't you? Your whole plan was built around a coming revolution."

"I can say this," J.J. said. "We are important, very important, and we have the support of what's left of the government and of all the services."

o 10 o

The approach to Mars was always an exciting experience for Dom. The negligible atmosphere of the planet allowed a clear view of the surface. A dust storm was blowing in a cyclonic pattern west of the Hellas plains in the southern hemisphere. The film of ice deposits in the northern polar area gleamed, a white jewel atop the globe. Doris was by his side, keeping an avid eye on the viewers, since it was her first trip to Mars.

Although she was arid, cruel, deadly to an unprotected man, Mars was Dom's second home. In recent years he'd spent as much time there as he had on Earth. He was proud to be a part of a service which made human presence on Mars possible, and he was bitter because events on Earth now threatened, more than ever, the developments which had been scratched and dug out of the planet at the cost of much labor and some human life.

During the days in which he watched the planet grow from a bright star into a disc and then into a huge, dominating sphere hanging over the *Kennedy*, he talked with Doris about his feelings. Mars policy was made on Earth, and it was contradictory and confused.

"Take the *Kennedy*," he said. "For what she cost we could have supplied plenty of water for the entire planet for all time."

He pointed out the ice deposits at the north pole.

"There's enough water there to change the face of the planet," he said. "If all the water in the ice deposits could be released, the planet would be covered in water to a depth of ten meters, about thirty feet. That's a theoretical figure, and it would be accurate only if the planet were a smooth globe. The point is, we've spent billions building this ship to carry water out here and all the time there's plenty of water already here if we had the money and the manpower to develop it."

Mars was anything but a smooth planet. The huge shield volcano, Olympus Mons, showed on the horizon. Even from height and distance Olympus Mons was impressive.

"Two and a half times as high as Everest," Dom said. "Fifteen miles high."

"Quite a mountain," Doris said. "I don't think I'd want to try to climb it."

"It's not all that tough," Dom said. "Remember, it's less than half Earth gravity. The only tough part of the climb is in lower altitudes, because of the winds. I've seen winds of two hundred miles per hour on the lower slopes. But no one climbs the thing. It's too easy to take a jumper and set it down on the peak. If we find the time I'll take you up. I think you'd enjoy it."

From space, Mars looked like a planet stripped down to its skeleton. An ancient riverbed, with tributaries branching out like small veins from an artery, lanced across a flat plain pimpled by meteorite craters. The effects of the Martian wind could be seen in the dark tails extending outward from the craters, marking the deposit of bright dust particles. As the rotation of the planet brought the canyon area into view, Doris was, again, impressed. The giant rift covered an area as long as the distance from New York to San Francisco. The main chasm, Tithonius Chasma, would have made the Grand Canyon of the Colorado look like a small creekbed. The stark and terrible beauty of the planet misted Doris' eyes. She leaned against Dom, her hand on his arm.

"I once hated her," Doris said.

"Why?" he asked, not thinking.

"Because she took you away from me."

"That was a long time ago," he said.

"I can understand why she draws men," Doris said. "I can see why, once you've seen her, you have to come back."

"There are ten thousand people down there," Dom said, pointing out the high volcanic plains in the Elysium area. "They live in quarters which would give most Earthlings claustrophobia. They breathe reconstituted air which they've made themselves by breaking down the oxygen from rocks and what little water can be pumped from the ground. They're dependent on Earth for most of their food and manufactured materials. There are marvelous things on Mars, minerals, jewels, metals. She'll never have to worry about overpopulation, because she wasn't meant for man. But she can give to man. There's enough raw material there to ease a lot of shortages back on Earth. And what do we carry when we send a ship back? Fertilizer."

"I've always thought Mars policy was penny-wise and pound-foolish," Doris said.

"We have the technology right now to change the entire Martian environment," Dom said. "We could use the hydro engine to shift the two moons just a little, just enough to change the motion of the planet to give more sun heat at the poles. The caps would melt and the planet would be wetter, warmer, and that would make her almost self-sustaining."

"Can you imagine the screams from the nature worshipers?" Doris asked, with a laugh. "Can you imagine the lawsuits which would be filed if the department announced that it was going to change the sacred ecology of an entire planet?"

"The battle cry would be, 'Lichens Have Rights,' " Dom said.

The *Kennedy's* huge powerplant was thrusting against her motion, slowing her. Mars hung over the ship, huge, red, beautiful. Landing preparations went smoothly. Although the ship was huge, she had the power to go in and come up on her own in the light gravity of Mars. Neil put her down as if he were handling a scout ship a fraction of her size. Men began to offload the water, which would strain the storage capacity of the tanks. It would be a long job, since existing pumping facilities had been designed for much smaller quantities of water.

Dom introduced Doris to old friends, guided her through the museum to see the scanty remains of the primitive extinct animal and plant life. The museum always made him feel sad. It told its story only too well. Mars had once been a living planet, both geologically and biologically. Scientists were still discussing the cause of her death. Currently, the most favored theory pointed to a varying sun. That school of theorists said that tens or hundreds of millions of years in the past, the sun had radiated more energy. At that far-distant time, the water now encased in the polar icecaps had been free, the atmosphere more dense, the whole planet wetter, allowing the development of both plant and animal life.

Dom wasn't too happy with that theory. It could neither be proved nor disproved. The nature of a star is such that in a body the size of old Sol, energy released at the sun's core requires some eight million years to work its way to the surface, where it is then radiated to the planets within minutes. Activity at the suns surface, the light falling on Mars that day, represented what had happened inside the sun millions of years ago and provided no clue as to the activity at the core at the given moment. However, if Mars had been affected by a change in the sun's energies, the Earth would have felt the same effects. Of course, there was plenty of evidence of changing conditions on Earth, but the evidence was subject to a variety of interpretations.

Depending on one's personal choice, fossil ferns and corals in arctic areas could be explained in several different ways, solar variation and continental drift being the two most favored theories. Solar variation was in current favor, since that theory also served to explain the change in Mars from a living planet to a desert of waste with lichens the only form of life to be found when Trelawny first landed on the red sands.

Dom was not fully convinced of either theory to explain some things on Earth. The presence of mammoths in the ice of both Siberia and Alaska, some frozen so rapidly that their flesh was, after millions of years, used as food for sled dogs, had never been explained by advocates of either theory. In fact, most scientists simply choose to ignore the puzzle of the frozen mammoths.

Perhaps, Dom felt, the true explanation could involve a combination of both factors, plus some things not yet theorized. He, himself, could not guess at additional factors, but he believed that continental drift had a definite part. The evidence cited by those who studied plate tectonics was very convincing.

It was one thing to study the past on Earth, and another to see it in skeleton form on Mars, to see the pathetic remains of life as evidence that something, some terrible force, had turned a living planet into a dead one. The old, romantic notions of dead civilizations on

Mars were long since discredited, but there had been life, life very similar to that of the Earth, and all that life, except for some hardy lichens, had been wasted.

Doris seemed to sense Dom's mood of melancholy. She suggested a meal and coffee in the main cafeteria. It was good to be with people again, to hear the talk, to smell their presence.

The meal was cultured protein, the coffee hot and strong. They chatted with two phosphate miners seated at the next table, lingered over cigarettes, and then made their way topside for a jumper ride back to the *Kennedy.* The twenty-four-hour Martian day was ending as they boarded. Ellen and J.J. were on watch. They were eager to take their turn at going into the domes. It was merely changing one closed environment for another, but it was a change from shipboard life.

Alone on the ship, they sat in the control room, the view being better there, had a glass of their own personal alcohol ration, watched the small moons grow brighter in the swift darkness as the planet swung them into nightside. In the darkness, neither of them having activated the lighting system, Dom felt a growing awareness of Doris' nearness.

She came into his arms without protest. Her lips were sweet. He felt a new sense of possessiveness, a sense of wonder. She was his, his girl, his woman. The hostile world in front of the viewport seemed to emphasize their aliveness. They were alone, only their lives, their two separate entities, belying the dead world outside, the cold, airless surface. Far way, their own world was being torn apart, once again, in strife between men. Still farther away was a bloated gas giant with a killing, crushing gravity field and monstrous pressures. Strife and uncertainty behind them, danger ahead of them. The kiss reaffirmed the fact that they were, for the moment at least, alive. But there was an agreement between them.

He pushed her away, his breath rapid, his pulse pounding. "Girl, you'd better run for your life," he whispered.

"No fair," she said. "Don't try to force me to have enough willpower for two."

"Women are scarce on Mars," Dom said. "So they make things as simple as possible. There's no waiting period for marriage. We don't believe in wasting a single moment."

"Wonderful," she said.

"Huh?"

"All right, I'll make it perfectly clear," she said. "So that even a man can understand. Yes."

"Yes?" he asked.

"Y-e-s," she spelled. "Yes."

"You're sure?"

"Now you're sounding as though you're not sure," she said, hitting him lightly with her fist. "Look, I feel very, very small and very, very insignificant. I want reassurance. I guess I'm all female, because what I need is the safety and the security of your arms around me."

He held her happily for a few moments. Then he contacted ground control and stated his needs. The minister was aboard *Kennedy* within the hour, scarcely giving Doris time to put on her best uniform. The brief ceremony was witnessed, in the absence of the rest of *Kennedy's* crew, by two men from the landing-pad staff. The bride was toasted in clear, cold water.

Once again they were alone. There was, at first, a shyness between them. They were in Dom's quarters, since it was, as the captain's cabin, the larger. He helped her move her few personal possessions into the room, they used another bit of their wine ration, and came together to give mutual assurances against the long and lonely night outside. She was more than he remembered and all that he'd ever dreamed.

In the early morning Dom lay awake listening to her soft breathing. Now and then she made a tiny little purring sound. He felt a great welling up in his chest, and he smiled as he looked at her face. His eyes misted in sheer gladness.

The ship muttered and whispered around them. A servo cut in somewhere deep down, and he could feel the sense of well-being which comes from being on a living ship. The ship did have a sort of life. She functioned, giving herself orders through the complicated circuits, the miles of wiring. She lived and she allowed the crew to live. But only so long as man-made machinery did the job of purifying air.

He felt a fear. Doris, beside him, stirred in her sleep and one of her long, soft legs came over his, so smooth, so warm, so terribly vulnerable to the harsh and uncaring emptiness of space. Doris lived, but she lived only because the ship which he'd designed provided her with a suitable environment. As long as his hull held out cold and vacuum, as long as his hull resisted the crushing pressures of the Jovian atmosphere, she would continue to live.

It was not a prophecy. It was not an omen. He didn't believe in premonitions. The ship would take them there and it would bring them back. But had he made a mistake? Should they have waited? Having known the little hot slicknesses of her, the cling of her, the hunger of her lips and body, would he err on the side of overcaution, thinking of her?

So it must have been, he thought, in the first days, when the first man looked at his woman and desired her to the point of fear of losing her. So it was in the dawn-age civilizations, when the first cities offered some protection against the fierce and warring savages. Throughout history, and in prehistory, a man looked at his sleeping woman and knew the same fears, dreamed the same dreams, facing death but dreading its coming before the appointed time. Dawn-age man protected his woman from the beasts, from the desires of other men, and Dominic Gordon, lying awake in a huge spaceship on Mars, vowed to protect his woman from the hostile environment and from other men. He would protect her with fang and claw and with his skills, and he would take her into the high pressure of the Jovian clouds and expose her to great danger, and then if they lived they would face the renewed savagery of the barbarians of Earth. How he would protect her he was not sure, but he would. He would make a safe place for his woman, and for all women.

He went to sleep with fierce half-dreams of blood and killing, mentally devastating Firsters and Savers and all others who insisted on turning his planet into a bloody arena, fierce man dreaming of wrecking havoc on other fierce men.

As light grew on the eastern horizon the servos of the *Kennedy* compensated for temperature changes in the hull. The sun, shrunken by distance, was still a powerful force as it rose above the harsh and eroded mountains.

o 11 o

"I am shamelessly happy," Doris said.

The jumper sat atop the fifteen-mile height of the ancient crater, Olympus Mons.

"I will not feel guilty for being happy," she said.

"I know," he said.

The news from Earth was bad. In the west, terrorists were gaining steadily. The valuable space facility at DOSEWEX was besieged and was being sustained by airlift. There was talk of evacuating DOSEWEX, to concentrate the defense in the east. Should DOSEWEX be abandoned, everything of value would have to be destroyed. The waste would be horrifying. Moreover, with DOSEWEX gone, one lucky hit on the Houston center would leave DOSE without communications with its ships in space. J.J. sent down word to hold DOSEWEX at all costs.

DOSE was, of course, in command of the moon. A command post had been set up there. To compensate for the possible loss of DOSEWEX, powerful communications equipment had been lifted from the Canaveral base, and it was now possible for *Kennedy* to communicate directly with the command post.

Dom was surprised to find that J.J. was considered by those on the moon to be quite powerful and very valuable. J.J. received regular reports on the situation.

Although the situation was not good, it was encouraging that the vast masses of the people still seemed to be content to sit back and watch without taking sides. Both sides were leaning over backward to treat the populace with the utmost consideration. Refugees from battle zones were living in more luxury than most of the citizens who had not been driven from their homes. Both forces shared food and supplies and medical treatment with their refugees. The alliance between the remnants of government and the armed services had seized vast stores of materials and food and were less strained than the rebels.

At times the fighting was deadly and fierce, but the real battle was being fought in the minds of the uncommitted masses. The propaganda flow from both sides promised milk and honey in the future.

Dom knew exactly what Doris meant about feeling guilty. While the world faced the crisis, he found the days of waiting on Mars to be the happiest of his life. While they were not pulling watch they were free to explore. The trip to the top of the planet's highest mountain was only one of several excursions which they enjoyed while the water was being offloaded. Since a jumper is self-powered by the heat of the sun, it was not at all wasteful to travel. Dom was an old Mars hand, knew the best times to view the huge rift system to get a maximum show of light and shadow, knew the best vantage point atop Olympus Mons, and enjoyed it anew because of the delight which Doris showed.

There was time, during the waiting period, to talk with the crew of the *Callisto Explorer,* who had seen the alien ship dive into Jupiter. Those men had seen the ship, had heard the weak signals which were still being transmitted from just inside the gaseous atmosphere. On watch, Dom could speak directly to the picket ship on duty out near the gas giant. While keeping radio watch on the signals, the ship was taking atmosphere samples from the larger moons of Jupiter's thirteen-satellite system. Dom often talked with the skipper.

The signal was too weak to be picked up by *Kennedy's* receivers, but the picket ship could relay it. Dom made dozens of recordings for study. The alien was broadcasting on one of the natural frequencies, 1420 megahertz. The signal was simple and brief, so brief it still defied attempts at decoding. Still, he felt closer to the goal to be able to listen to the relay from the picket ship.

In talking with crew who had done picket duty, Doris was impressed by the words of one young spacer.

"When you're in close," he said, "she swallows up all of space and looms over your head so that you wake up in a cold sweat thinking that she's come unstuck and is falling down on top of you."

Every man who had been near Jupiter had been awed by her.

One of the things Dom liked best about Mars was the feeling of togetherness which permeated the population. Everyone felt the friendliness—temporary visitors, spacers, permanent settlers, scientists. The harshness of the surface, the millions of miles which separated them from home, the odd, small look of the sun, covering only two-thirds of the area of sky which an Earth-viewed sun covered, all seemed to draw people closer together. In spite of the armed guard which surrounded the *Kennedy* at all times, it was difficult to believe that the Earthside war could affect Mars. Dom expressed the belief that if a Firster fanatic could penetrate the service and get all the way to Mars he would be impressed that feel the sense of accomplishment shared by all spacers, would forget his beliefs and become just a spacer. That he was wrong was evidenced by an attempt to attach a limpet mine to the

Kennedy's number four port thruster by an enlisted spacer with twelve years' service. Caught in the act, the man took two space marines with him into the small but growing Mars Station Cemetery.

The incident seemed to kill the glow of contentment and happiness which Dom had felt since Doris said yes that night in the main control room. To think that the lunacy of Earth could contaminate Mars depressed him. He was glad when the hold was closed and pressurized and the *Kennedy* once again stood ready.

The longest leg of the journey lay ahead of them. Roughly, they had traveled one half of an astronomical unit to reach Mars, about one half the distance between Earth and the sun, or about forty-seven million miles. The distance between Mars and Jupiter was roughly three and three-quarters astronomical units, in the neighborhood of three hundred and sixty million miles. When dealing with such figures the mind refused to accept the vastness of space and tended to think of the journey in terms of months. Distance becomes relative when expressed in terms of time. Dom liked to remember that it had taken the pioneers almost as long to travel from the midwest to the Pacific coast by wagon train as it now took a ship to move from the orbit of Mars to the orbit of Jupiter. *Kennedy,* with her unlimited power for acceleration, was at her best over long distances. She could pick up speed faster, cruise faster, and slow faster than conventional ships.

After a thorough inspection of the ship, although no Mars personnel had boarded her, they settled into the comfortable routine which had been established during the last weeks of the run to Mars. Jensen's powerplant pushed and then rested. Acceleration continued well past the midway point. A picket ship was still on duty near Jupiter, and the watch on both ships, glad for company in the vastness of space, talked back and forth, using relatively low power as the distance between them grew steadily less, so that their often informal conversations could not be monitored back on Earth.

At turnaround time, Neil and Jensen swung the mass of the *Kennedy* and the reverse thrust began to kill the forward speed.

On Earth, the situation had reached an uneasy stability. Both sides had suffered heavy casualties. The defense line was holding on the Chicago–Corpus Christi line, and DOSEWEX was holding out. The propaganda war was still raging, and the masses were beginning to mutter about the shortage of food and consumer goods. Some of the most severe battles had been fought in the grain belt of the great plains. Large areas of fertile farmland had been devastated. There would be difficulty in planting spring crops.

It was no longer possible to brush off the senator from New Mexico with contempt, for he had emerged as the man who was clearly in control of the radical forces, and he was now more often than not referred to by his name, John V. Shaw. He had proved himself to be not only a skillful organizer, but a brilliant military tactician. Shaw was preaching the gospel of revolt to the masses, promising to pull in all the slackers from space, to beat the spaceship hulls into plowshares in order to produce food under a new form of freedom. The exact form of this new freedom was not spelled out. It was clear, however, that the senator's message was a vital one as food supplies became more and more scarce.

It seemed to the crew of the *Kennedy* that it was only a matter of time before the hungry millions began to flock to Shaw's cause. Starvation is the most powerful of persuasions, and vast segments of the metropolitan east faced severe hunger as winter approached.

Time was critical. J.J. talked of a swift completion of their mission, a long run home, an arrival during the Christmas season.

"I think you're being optimistic, J.J.," Dom said. "You're allowing only a short time for the descent into the atmosphere, the location of the ship, and bringing her out."

"We'll do it," J.J. said.

"It's a big planet," Art said.

"We can home in on the radio signal," J.J. said. "We won't have any trouble locating the ship."

"There's always trouble in a new situation," Neil said. "Keep in mind that we'll be testing a new and untried ship under severe conditions."

"What's to test?" J.J. asked. "It's a very simple proposition. She does it or she doesn't. She goes in. That much we know. She'd have to go in to test the hull, so why fool around? We go in. If she doesn't implode, we come out. Why worry?"

"That's fine to say," Ellen said.

"We will not dive in without testing the hull," Dom said in a firm voice. J.J. looked at him. "I'm not going to lower myself to the level of a Firster," Dom said. "I value my life. I value each life aboard this ship. So we'll poke our nose in, test the compression qualities of the hull, and then we'll lower in easy stages."

"And if every little thing doesn't please you?" J.J. asked.

"My decision," Dom said. "I will take the responsibility."

"I just wonder if it would be worth going back if we fail," J.J. said.

"It's human to cling to life even when there is no hope," Dom said.

"Especially if you've just been married," J.J. said.

Dom looked at J.J. levelly. "I resent that, J.J. My

private life is my own as long as it doesn't keep me from performing my duties. I defy you to point out one instance of my private considerations having affected my judgment or the performance of my duties."

"Sorry, Flash," J.J. said. "I'm worried, that's all."

"We all are," Doris said.

Dom set the crew to work on dry runs of making the descent run. It was a little early, but they were getting edgy and the rehearsals kept them busy. Privacy time was cut. Dom and Doris deliberately avoided being alone together, as if to prove to the others that their changed status did not affect performance.

Three days before time to go into orbit around the gas giant, the *Kennedy's* RDF locked onto the signal from the alien ship. It seemed to be a miracle that the signal was still steady, still the same strength as it was so long ago when the *Kennedy* was nothing more than a dream and some often-conflicting data in the DOSEWEX computer. The fact that the ship was still down there, beeping away, reinforced the theory that she was trapped and incapable of escaping the gravitational and atmospheric fields of the giant planet.

"If there is anyone or anything aboard her," Art said, "he, she, or it will be happy to see us."

Doris was very busy in those last days before going into orbit. She checked and rechecked all data. The task of putting the ship into orbit and then lowering her gently, oh so gently, into the fringe of atmosphere was Doris' baby. Her fingers and data from the shipboard computer had to be right, had to feed the right information into the automatics and to Neil.

They passed the last picket ship and received a good luck from the crew. As space distances go, they were right next door to the smaller ship, but they did not get a visual on her. The picket ship would stay on orbit to observe as *Kennedy* went down.

They were there. The mass of Jupiter covered half of space. Moons were visible to the naked eye. The ship moved swiftly around the planet, subjected to radiation, the electrical field, the gravity of the giant. *Kennedy* functioned flawlessly.

Because of the speed of Jupiter's spin, and the vast forces of her gravity, *Kennedy* would have to go in very, very hot. Power would be constant to counteract the gravity. When last-minute drills had been performed there was no formal order. The computer picked the time and Neil's hands did not touch the controls as the ship began to spiral down.

She was dwarfed by the mass of the planet, a mass which measured two and a half times as heavy as all the other planets of the solar system combined. Slowly, slowly, she went down toward that roiling surface, speed and power and rate of fall regulated by Doris' computer. Those inside her had the feeling of falling into a hell of bright yellow fire as they orbited on the sunside and began to see with the naked eye the giant hurricane in the southern tropical zone, the Giant Red Spot, blowing for centuries at a force of hundreds of miles per hour.

The bands of atmosphere showed tremendous wind shears as atmospheric movement tossed and buffeted the insignificant mass of the ship. Each of them was aware, as the ship went down and down, that should their power fail, the ship would be seized by the massive gravitational force, yanked through the thin layer of outer clouds to drop, pulled by a force of three Earth gravities, the pressure outside building as they fell through a zone of frozen ammonia crystals, then into liquid ammonia and the zone of colored compounds which gave the atmosphere its distinctive yellow covering. They would, as they were being pulled inexorably downward, pass frozen crystals of ice and then a zone of water vapor, and they would all be dead before the crushed remains of the ship fell into the zone of liquid molecular hydrogen and continued to be compressed as pressures mounted to three million atmospheres at the transition zone between liquid molecular hydrogen and liquid metallic hydrogen, and the temperature would be rising to melt the remains of the tiny Earth ship and the even smaller, more thoroughly crushed Earth people.

On a model of the planet the size of an apple, the zone of operation of the *Kennedy* could be represented by the thickness of the apple's skin. Below that very thin layer of operations lay instant death as the hull imploded.

The size of the monster! It was psychologically suffocating. It swallowed the whole of space from the viewports. It had the weight of a sun which failed. It was of incredible mass. It loomed above them as down became up and they felt dizzied. Ellen hid her eyes in her hands as the giant reached out for them with pressure and gravity and electromagnetic discharges registered by the sensors. The *Kennedy* went down near the orbit of the innermost moon, Amalthea. The moon was above them now, and slightly ahead, the ship between the moon's orbit and the uppermost layer of cloud. A vast discharge of electricity came, lighting the area between the small moon and the planet, soundless in vacuum, but bright, sudden, startling, and, had the ship been struck, deadly. Again, as Dom held his breath, the tremendous bolt leaped from planet to moon.

"I think it's trying to tell us something," Neil said, in an awed voice.

"Old Jove, the god of lightning," J.J. said. "He's saying, 'Look on my majesty, you puny mortals, and despair.'"

"I didn't know you had a poetic soul," Dom said.

Dom was moved by the vastness of the Jovian mass. It was heavy over him, seemingly over his head, and the *Kennedy* went down, measuring herself in a thousand ways as she lowered. Hull sensors sent the first recognition of faint traces of atmosphere. Slowly, slowly. She was doing well. Instruments worked and measured and gave their readings and the computer hummed and now scattered molecules of frozen ammonia made for a gradual lessening of vision. The *Kennedy* continued to fall into a murky sea of crystals. Her hull melted crystals. Temperature was going up, but it was well within operational levels.

"Level her off," Dom ordered, when the outside pressure was one Earth atmosphere.

Neil took over from the automatics, to get the feel of the ship in case of systems failure. The ship was in a stationary orbit, moving with the surface rotation. Pressure was as predicted.

It was time to test one of the ship's most crucial weapons for doing battle with the gas giant. Dom ordered two atmospheres in the living compartments. He felt his ears pop as the pressure built. Huge pumps moved clean air from the hold, and to take its place in the hold compartments, the poisonous atmosphere of Jupiter was let in.

Satisfied that the internal pressure system was working properly, Dom ordered a descent until pressure equalized. And then, time after time, the process was repeated. In the murky atmosphere the ship saw only by her instruments, keeping position directly above the alien ship, guided by the continuing signal. That signal, that ship down there, that was the purpose of it all. It had drawn them onward, had inspired a last-ditch crucial effort on the part of the space industry. Only that signal and what was sending it justified the cost of the

Kennedy, the risk involved, the use of scarce materials.

And the signal stopped when the *Kennedy* was only six atmospheres deep into the clouds.

The *Kennedy* became, in that sudden silence, a dinosaur. She had no purpose.

"Check equipment," Dom ordered.

"All check," Doris said.

"Check manual," Dom said. "Hold this position."

He himself ran a manual check on the receiver. It was operational. A radio check with the picket ship confirmed that the signal from the alien had suddenly ceased.

"Damn," Dom said. "We were halfway there." That was in distance, not in pressure. "We'll hold here for a few hours. Maybe it will start up again."

Four hours passed, during which the ship functioned perfectly. There was no break of the radio silence from the alien ship.

"Maybe he heard us coming and doesn't want company?" Doris asked.

"No, it just went dead," J.J. said. "It's a damned miracle it has lasted so long. The ship's still there."

"For all the good it does," Dom said.

"We have its position," J.J. said. "We can lower down right on top of it."

"Not likely," Neil said. "Even under power these winds move us around. Without the signal it would be only a guess to put us within a hundred miles of her."

"The descent is predicted on the computer," J.J. said. "We can estimate corrections. We can get within a few miles and do a search."

"We might find her if we had a hundred years to look," Dom said.

"All we have is time," J.J. said. "We have the power. We have air and supplies."

"J.J., we built this ship for staying a limited time in

three thousand atmospheres," Dom said. "After ten days I wouldn't want to bet against metal fatigue in the mush bondings."

"All right, we have ten days," J.J. said. "We can at least use it."

"We can at least gather some interesting data," Art said.

"I want to point out that we will be exposing this ship and her crew to unnecessary danger," Neil said. "It is my opinion that going deeper into the atmosphere is now useless. If I were in her alone I'd take her down to three thousand atmospheres just to test the design, but I'm not alone. It's one thing to risk the life of a professional test pilot in experimentation, another to risk the lives of a crew."

"We hold for one more hour," Dom said.

It was a tense hour, and when it was over J.J. paced the control room fretfully. Dom had spent the hour with Doris, directing her through some calculations.

"J.J.," he said, "if we had one chance in a thousand of finding the ship I'd take her down, but I've run it through and the odds are a billion to one against finding her. I've also done some calculations on the length of stay at three thousand atmospheres. After eight days, the chances of failure increase to a point of risk. I think we're worth more alive, and the ship is worth something for the Mars run. In short, I'm giving the order to take her up and out."

"Then I am forced to ask you to relinquish your command," J.J. said.

"No," Dom said quietly. "I am in command. I built her and I know her limitations."

"You have no choice," J.J. said. "As your superior officer, I hereby inform you that I am taking command. Mr. Walters, make preparations to take her down to three thousand atmospheres."

"With all due respect, sir, I decline," Neil said. "I don't agree that Captain Gordon should be removed from command."

J.J. was facing them, his hands behind his back. He looked down at his feet, turned slowly, hands still clasped behind his back. He stood there, his back to them, for a long time, and then he turned quickly, his hand moving to point a small but deadly splatter gun at them. The weapon was designed for close-in killing in delicate areas. The blast of multiple projectiles could be fatal to anyone within a few feet, but there was not enough force behind the projectiles to, for example, hole the hull of a ship.

"I'm sorry it's come to this," J.J. said. "But we're going to do the job we came out here to do."

"Not this way," Dom said.

"You leave me no choice."

"You're one against six," Neil said. "You can't stay awake forever."

"J.J.," Dom said, "put that thing away. If you're so convinced that we should go down, we'll go down. We came out here together. We'll go down together."

"You have my sincere thanks," J.J. said.

"Gun or no gun, we'll stay down no longer than seven days. Is that clear?" Dom asked.

"I agree," J.J. said.

"Is everyone in agreement?" Dom asked. "We take the ship down to do what she was designed to do instead of risking someone's getting killed if we try to overpower J.J.?"

"I am shocked," Doris said, "but I'm for going down."

The others agreed.

"Stations," Dom said. "We're going down. We won't come up with anything but a few million cubic feet of

Jovian atmosphere in the hold, but I intend to see that we do come up."

They did it slowly and carefully. The crew worked smoothly, the incident with J.J. seemingly forgotten. Dom had to admit to himself that he'd wanted to go down all along. Fully alive, moving into an area where man had never been, he could almost feel the pressure on the hull as he rode herd on his instruments and the ship sank, buffeted by winds of hundreds of miles per hour, only the brute power of the drive holding the *Kennedy* against them. Only once did the ship drop down a wind sheer before the automatics compensated.

The hull sensors told of the changing atmosphere. Frozen ammonia became liquid ammonia, and then they were in the zone of the yellow compounds. Always, inexorably, the pressure built. At two thousand atmospheres the air inside the ship seemed to be sticky, heavy, oppressive. But the ship reacted sweetly to the incredible forces, the mush-bonded seams compressing, folding, the instruments recording within the limits of safety on all hull areas.

Signals went out from the ship, seeking, searching. They found nothing but increasing density of atmosphere. The danger below was beyond imagination. The distance traveled, as the ship orbited, matching the speed of rapid rotation, was not a factor. The winds of Jupiter blew against them with a solid force. And her gravity tugged on them, always ready to seize them, should the power fail, and pull them toward the core of the planet.

The living compartments of the ship were now between two pressures, the outside weight of atmosphere and the compressed bulk of Jovian atmosphere inside the hold. *Kennedy* had multiplied her weight by taking in the Jovian gases, but the power plant was not even strained.

At three thousand atmospheres Neil began a search, swinging the ship back and forth at the same altitude.

Preliminary analysis of the atmosphere at three thousand atmospheres showed an interesting array of hydrogen and carbon compounds, confirming advance theory that such matter made up the bulk of the yellow layers of Jupiter. In order to obtain pure samples of the yellow layer, the hold was bled and cleaned of the noxious ammonia taken in at the upper levels.

The search continued without success. J.J. took a personal interest in venting the poisonous gases and liquids from the hull, leaving only material collected under maximum pressure in the yellow zone. He seemed to be much too cheerful for conditions, for the search for the alien had produced nothing. When he was satisfied that the huge hold contained only yellow-layer material he came into the control room with a pleased grin on his face.

"Flash, you can take her home anytime you're ready," he said.

It had taken three Earth days to vent and fill the hold. "We've got a few days left," Dom said.

"We've got what we came for," J.J. said.

Dom wondered if the strain had blown his mind. "I don't see signs of an alien ship in the hold," he said.

"There is no alien," J.J. said.

"Want to repeat that?" Dom asked.

"There never was an alien," J.J. said. "The signal came from an Explorer class ship, a drone."

"At three thousand atmospheres?" Dom asked, examining J.J. closely.

"At a mere ten atmospheres," J.J. said.

"But the picket ships measured—" Dom began.

"What their instruments were rigged to measure," J.J. said. "And the transmissions were halted on my orders."

"I'm trying to understand some of this," Dom said grimly. Neil was listening with a frown on his face. "You're telling me we built this ship just to come out here and get a load of Jovian muck?"

"We came out here to win a war," J.J. said. "Now as I read your specifications, we can vent the load in the hold down to an interior pressure of two thousand atmospheres and go home."

"I'm waiting for an explanation," Dom said.

"Did you ever read the Bible?" J.J. asked, grinning.

"Some."

"Remember the part about manna, my boy? Manna from heaven?"

Well, he was obviously mad. Dom felt a heavy weight of sadness. It was all for nothing. All the work, the brushes with death, the death of Larry, those terrible moments when he felt sure the Firster bomb would go off in his hands before he could jettison it into space, all of it had been done for the sake of a man who was obviously mad.

Manna from heaven. Venus torn full-grown from Jove's brow.

"Neil," Dom said, suddenly feeling very tired, "let's take her home."

"Roger," Neil said, looking at J.J. with a mixture of puzzlement and anger.

o 12 o

The ship faced one final test. She had passed many tests to bring them millions of miles on a madman's quest. She had lifted thousands of tons of water out of the moon's gravity well. She had brought them through space, and she had resisted the force of pressure. The last test was as crucial as any. If she failed to fight her way upward and beyond the gravity of the gas giant, all the others didn't count.

Until now her power had been used only to neutralize gravitational attraction in orbit. Now she was called upon to overcome the pull and apply enough force to the hull to move upward and then to attain escape velocity, at more than twice the speed it would have taken her to leave Earth. Most important, she had to stay in one piece, and, if the madman was to be humored, she had to do it with thousands of tons of Jovian atmosphere in her hold.

The computer gave angle of climb, increments of power, times, and the automatics fed it into the engine. Neil followed the motions with his hands, just to get the feel of it. There was a different pitch to the quiet background hum inside her. The acceleration was slight at first. Only instruments could feel it. The ship mushed slowly upward. Full speed could not be attained in the drag of the atmosphere. The upward flight was slow and tedious. It was monitored by thousands of instruments ranging from hull-temperature gauges to nutrino traps measuring the efficiency of the hydroplant.

She was a pure thing of joy, Neil was thinking. He'd flown every type of ship built in the United States and some that were built elsewhere. He'd never flown anything like this one.

"You're a helluva ship builder," he told Dom with a grin.

Dom smiled ruefully. Being praised by a man like Neil was pleasant, but it was small compensation. There was, of course, the pride which comes when your own ideas and work bear fruit and prove a successful design. There wasn't another ship like *Folly*.

Revealing, of course, that he was thinking of her not as the *J.F.K.*, but as *Folly*. *J.J.'s Folly*.

The tension in the control room was not all engendered by the ticklish task of lifting the ship out of the atmosphere into clear space without straining the laden hull, without burning a thruster tube with too much power. Actually, the lifting went on so long it became routine. It was J.J.'s presence which caused most of the tension. Dom felt a sick disappointment. He had not realized, until the moment of J.J.'s surprise announcement, that he'd been counting heavily on that alien ship. There was a personal element in his disappointment. He had been duped into going on the ultimate treasure hunt, a sublight drive the potential reward, and all the time there had been no treasure. He had been promised the stars, and the payload was Jovian soup, thick soup compressed inside *Folly's* cargo hold.

In the ideal world, *Folly* could have been built in the interest of pure research, to prove that it could be done, to obtain samples of Jovian atmosphere, to merely add to knowledge. In an ideal world, however, there would also be plenty of food. That situation had not existed on the world for decades.

Idle thoughts as the ship lifted. From a long-range viewpoint, pure research paid off. The hydrogen engine which powered the *Folly* had roots in the early space program. Photographs taken during the first Skylab experiment, a pure research project, gave astrophysicists new and startling information about the sun. Questions raised about traditional ideas of the sun's power way back in the 1970s led to the breakthrough which allowed *Folly* to rise against the force of Jovian gravity. Had not scientists doing pure research work at an observatory in Arizona discovered that the sun's entire globe pulsated, the theories which made the hydrogen drive a reality would have been left unformulated. From a long-range point of view, Skylab was worthwhile, but even then there were people who screamed against the expenditure and wanted, instead, to buy butter, or welfare Cadillacs, for that group of nonachievers who are always a festering portion of human society.

Reactionary thinking, he told himself. The poor are always with us. He was not right-wing enough to be able to forget them, especially in view of the fact that he would soon be one of them, in the same boat with the starving millions. Where had it all gone wrong? All he wanted was to work in space, perhaps do a little bit to help halt man's galloping breeding, perhaps, eventually, to help man escape the overcrowded planet into richer pastures.

The man who built the *Folly* was feeling guilty. Enough money had been spent building her to expand the mining on Mars tenfold, to produce enough phosphates to fertilize half of the farmlands of the world. An achievement in pure science had come at the expense of many more needed projects. Once the whole story of *Folly* was known, the impact would kill the space program. Even if the civil war was won by government forces there would continue to be criticism of *Folly* as long as man hungered for food.

For a moment Dom wondered if it wouldn't be best for the hull to fail or a thruster to burn, leaving *Folly* to perish, never to be seen by human eyes again. But to have *Folly* plunge into the depths of Jupiter would not erase the knowledge that she had been built. Dead or alive, the ship, the ultimate achievement of the Department of Space Exploration, would be the instrument used by opponents of space spending to cripple the program for decades, perhaps forever.

The man who had engineered *Folly* went to his cabin as Neil brought her out into space through the thinning zone of frozen ammonia. From his bunk, he felt the power which sent the ship swooping upward and outward past the lonely moons, so powerful she did not feel the burden of Jovian soup in her hold.

He could not hide from his part in it. He went back into the control room. He called the picket ship and said, "It's over. We're headed home. Do you have fuel for Mars?"

"Affirmative," came the reply. "Congratulations, *J.F.K.*"

Dom made a grimace and did not acknowledge. He could feel the acceleration. He was tired. As far as he was concerned the ship could be put on auto and left to her own devices. At the moment he didn't care much about anything. He was thinking of the war, American killing American. He tried to gauge the impact of the news that the *Folly's* mission, made possible by the expenditure of billions, was a waste. The news could not be suppressed for long. An organization which could plant a fanatic on Mars, DOSE's most secure stronghold, could ferret out the news that *Folly* had been sent on a fool's errand and had come back with a load of noxious things from deep inside Jupiter.

He went back to his quarters and fell heavily onto his bunk. Doris was still at station and would be there until the flight plan was finalized and double-checked. When he heard a knock on his door he didn't answer, but the door was not locked.

J.J. stuck his head in. "Want to talk a minute, Flash?"

"I'd rather not right now," Dom said.

J.J. closed the door behind him. "It was a dirty trick, wasn't it?"

"J.J., just get out, huh?"

"In a minute." J.J. sat down. "Would it make you feel better to take a poke at me?"

"Don't tempt me."

"I wouldn't even put you on report," J.J. said. "Are you ready to listen, or are you still feeling sorry for yourself?"

"Do I have a choice?" Dom growled.

"You got the idea, didn't you?"

"Yes," Dom said. "I got it. My God, J.J., you faked an alien ship and spent billions of dollars to chase a fairy tale."

"I had to fake the ship," J.J. said. "I had to do something so that practical types, like you, could relate to it. I thought the idea was rather brilliant, didn't you?"

"J.J., I'm damned tired. Why don't you go take a nap?"

"Who would have listened if I'd told them the real reason?" J.J. asked. "It took a powerful incentive, like the prospect of finding a free sublight drive, to get anyone to listen."

"Yes," Dom said wearily.

"No need to put into Mars on the way home, huh?"

"No."

"We go in Moon Base, darkside."

"What difference does it make? Wherever we put her down she probably won't ever lift off again."

"She'll lift," J.J. said, "and dozens of others like her."

"Go away," Dom said.

"Promise me one thing."

"I don't know if I can."

"Promise me that no matter what you won't dump the cargo. Promise me that."

"What difference does it make?" Dom asked. "OK, we'll haul it back. It'll make a fine temporary cloud when we dump it out behind the moon."

"I've got something better to do with the cargo," J.J. said.

"Sure," Dom said, "you can supply the last two living scientists with enough Jovian atmosphere to last the few remaining days of their lifetimes, until the mobs catch them and tear their arms off."

J.J. was standing. "I can see you're a nonbeliever. Look up, boy. Peace and plenty lie ahead."

Dom heard the click of the door. He dozed and was wakened by the communicator.

It was Neil. "J.J. is calling a crew meeting in the lounge. I thought you'd want to listen."

"Might as well," Dom said. He splashed water into his eyes and walked heavily, still tired, through the half gravity of the corridors. He checked in at control. The ship was on auto. She was a good ship. Behind them, visible on the stern viewers, was the mass of Jupiter. It was still an awesome sight. He felt a flash of pride in having, in a small way, conquered the mass of the second-largest object in the solar system, but his pride faded quickly.

He made one final visual check on instruments. The autos were clicking and humming nicely, making mere man unnecessary, running the ship with a precision which man could never match. He walked toward the lounge slowly, dreading to see J.J. reveal his madness further.

The door was open. He halted just outside and heard Doris laugh. Neil was seated so that he could face the lounge instrument board, thus keeping his eye on important ship's functions. Doris was standing beside J.J. at the bar, serving drinks from J.J.'s personal bottle. They were all there except Jensen. Dom stood outside and watched. Ellen accepted a drink. Doris laughed at something Ellen said. They all drank and laughed. Nero, fidding while Rome burned around him. Dom didn't want to face it.

Still, sooner or later the others would have to hear the full story. He went in, resolved to see it through, then he changed his mind. Jensen wasn't there, and if they were not all there to hear it it would be told again, and one more telling was all Dom could stand.

He had passed through control only a couple of minutes before, but it was automatic to look around. His eyes made a scan and halted on a trouble light. Alerted, he punched the scan and was relieved to find that the problem was with nothing more important than the venting system in the hold. It wouldn't hurt to lose a few tons of Jupiter into space. He activated the self-examination system. The problem was in the control-room panel. He lifted a section and smelled burning insulation. It was nothing serious. All important systems were redundant. Even the venting system had backup. Down in the atmosphere, the venting system was all-important. He punched a complete check and got a second trouble light. Strange, but still not serious. When a third system went red in the stern section, a system designed for manual venting in the unlikely event that both venting systems went haywire, he got suspicious. The odds against two systems going out together were astronomical, but it had happened in space. For three to go without help was a little weird. He was not overly concerned yet, as he went toward the stern with the double purpose of finding Jensen and of checking to see what the hell had happened to the venting system. It was not a critical malfunction, or he would have alerted the crew. The shorted circuits in the central control room could be repaired easily, and the other malfunctions could be repaired at leisure, since the venting system would not be needed until they had reached the moon and received word to dump the useless cargo into space. He would merely check back in the stern, gather up Jensen, and then return to the lounge to allow J.J. to tell his pathetic story.

His deck shoes made his progress silent in the long corridor alongside the hold. The safety doors leading into the aft compartments were closed. He went into the lock, opened the last set of doors, and stepped into the forward engine compartment. Jensen was facing him, a spatter gun pointing its flared muzzle at his chest. Behind Jensen his board showed the venting system in red. Now Dom knew that if he could look out, he'd see the contents of the hold spewing out under great pressure into space.

"What the hell, Paul?" he asked, halting in mid-stride, careful not to make a sudden move. It was the second time in recent days he'd been in front of a spatter gun.

"You're supposed to be in the lounge," Paul said.

"Paul, isn't one nut on board enough?" He smiled disarmingly. "What's your problem?"

"I rather liked you, Dom," Jensen said, and Dom saw the preliminary tightening of Jensen's finger as he threw himself aside, hit the floor rolling as a spatter load smacked deck and bulkhead. He took a pellet on the ankle as the gun fired a second time, and he was still moving, no pain yet to indicate a hit, as he lifted a cleaning robot and, falling away behind a console, threw the heavy robot at Jensen. Jensen lifted his gun hand to try to block the robot. It struck him a glancing blow. Dom was diving toward him, moving up and under the gun, as the robot clanged off the deck and Jensen started lowering the gun to take aim. Dom had his hand on the wrist of the gun hand as they went down.

Jensen was surprisingly strong. Once the gun exploded inches away from Dom's ear, leaving his ear ringing with the concussion. With a climactic effort, he pinned the gun hand to the deck. Jensen landed a blow and Dom saw stars for a moment as his nose flattened and started spewing blood. Jensen pulled free, leaving the gun on the floor. Dom got to his feet. Jensen was standing by the control panel.

"Make a move, Gordon," Jensen panted, "and the whole ship goes." He had his hand on the manual drive control. "I've got the safeties bypassed. I can overload the plant and she'll become a real bomb."

"You'll die with the rest of us," Dom said.

"I don't want anyone to die."

"What do you want?"

"A couple of hours. Just long enough to empty the hold."

"Why is that so damned important?" Dom asked. "Are you crazy, too?"

"Why? Because the whole system is corrupt," Jensen said. "Because it's time for a change."

"You've blown your cover for nothing, Paul," Dom said. "But then I've always thought Firsters were crazy."

"You're the stupid one," Paul said. "Now listen. I

don't want to die, not now that we're winning, but I will if necessary. I want you to walk slowly over there, pick up the gun by the barrel, and hand it to me."

"May I say something first?"

"Make it quick."

"Paul, I don't give a damn if you empty the hold. Can you believe that? I couldn't care less. I'm not about to die just to try to save a sample of Jupiter's atmosphere. It would be interesting to analyze it, but I don't want to die either, and especially not for scientific curiosity. So do me a favor and don't panic, huh? Don't do anything silly. You're probably right when you say you're winning. Once this ship gets back she'll probably never go into space again. J.J. did more to kill space than all of you Firsters have done in fifty years. When you take over the country, you should give J.J. a medal. The point is, the damage is done. Let's all go home together, huh?"

"Do as I say, then."

"All right. I'm moving slow and easy. No tricks." He picked up the gun and began to straighten.

"One quick move and I'll blow her," Jensen said.

"Yes, I know," Dom said. "I'm moving slow." He walked very slowly, holding the gun by its muzzle in front of him. Jensen watched nervously, licking his lips. He kept one hand on the lever which, if he really had bypassed the safeties, would send the drive into a cataclysm which would make the *Kennedy* into a small temporary star.

"Here it is," he said. "Take it." Jensen looked down, leaned slightly forward. Off balance, he'd have to make two moves to throw the level to full on. No man alive could make two moves while Dom was making one. Dom flipped the gun, caught it, and triggered it, even as Jensen saw and tried to recover. The charge took Jensen's hand off at the wrist, the bloody stump completing the move which would have killed them all. Jensen's mouth opened to scream. The sound began, and in his shock and pain he showed good training, for his other arm reached for the lever, almost contacted the lever before Dom's second shot took him full in the face. There was no need for a third shot.

Dom stood for a moment, looking down to see that death was not instantaneous. The creature writhing in terminal pain no longer looked like a man.

Dom made a quick survey of the venting board. Only a fraction of the cargo had been dumped. He closed the vents and began checking to see if Jensen had really bypassed the safeties on the drive. The door opened, and Neil and J.J. rushed in.

"We're OK," Dom said. "Just don't try to add power until we've done some repairs."

"What happened?" Neil asked.

"He was dumping J.J.'s Jovian soup," Dom said. "He was a Firster."

With a cry of alarm, J.J. leaped to the venting board, checking the contents of the hold. When he saw that only a small part of the cargo was gone, he said, "I owe you again, Flash."

"I didn't do it to save your soup," Dom said. "I did it because I was not about to leave my life and the lives of the others in the hands of a nut."

"You'll get that promotion, Flash," J.J. said.

"Go go hell," Dom said. "You and Art clean this up." He indicated the body. "I'll help Neil make repairs."

Ellen pitched in and was not a bad hand with a tool. The work gave Dom something to take his mind off J.J.'s madness. When they were finished, several hours later, he was tired and dirty and wanted a bath and ten hours' sleep. He was almost into the second half of the program when J.J. came in, uninvited.

"Jensen is in cold storage. There'll be an inquiry when we get home."

Dom nodded.

"I've spent some time in the galley, Flash."

Dom sat up. J.J. extended a tray from a server which had been concealed behind him. Dom took a cup of coffee.

"Sugar, cream?" J.J. asked politely.

Dom shook his head.

"Try this with it," J.J. said, lifting the top of a silver server. On the tray inside were small pieces of something which looked very much like butter.

"What is it?"

"Just try it." J.J. picked up a small piece and popped it into his mouth.

Dom picked up a piece and looked at it. It had a slightly grainy texture. It had the spongy feel of a good, rich bread. He nibbled it tentatively, then took a bite and chewed thoughtfully. It was unlike anything he'd ever eaten. It had a wholesome, hearty taste, a pleasing richness.

"Do you want to listen to me for a minute now, Flash?" J.J. asked, grinning broadly.

"J.J.," Dom said, "I have to admit that you have my full attention."

o 13 o

Carbohydrates are not the most healthful of foods, when taken as a major portion of the diet, but a hungry man doesn't concern himself with nutrition, only with filling his belly. Carbohydrates are easily utilized by the body. They can supply a quick burst of energy, especially if rich in sugars. The blood sugar level rises immediately, and the eater feels a surge of energy.

Rationing was necessary at first, but, when added to the dwindling store of food stocks under the control of the government, the tons of carbohydrates which were ferried from the moon to Earthside turned the tide in the battle for the stomachs of the people.

At first, not too much care was taken about sanitation. Foodstuff was being delivered to fighting men on short rations and to civilians who didn't care too much about cleanliness, as long as the roughly carved chunks tasted good.

Later, as the country began to come back to normal and the forces of the Shaw Alliance were gradually pushed back into southern California and exterminated ruthlessly, the stuff was delivered in sanitary wrappings, carefully weighed, but available in plenty.

By the time Admiral Dominic Gordon returned from Jupiter with another load of raw material, there was a functioning government. Small amounts of the foodstuff went a long way, because it was rich. When released from the pressurized hold of the *John F. Kennedy,* the stuff expanded into tons and tons of richness.

The space industry had new life. War damage slowed the recovery, but space was a high-priority field. A second Kennedy class ship was being built out beyond the moon. Plans for the ship were given to the governments of the U.K., Japan, Germany, and the U.S.S.R., and within months they had their own tankers under construction. There was plenty of room out beyond the moon.

It was not all generous and selfless, the donation of the research which went into the *Kennedy,* and the distribution, without cost, of tons of rich carbohydrates to India, Africa, and Asia. No one gets something for nothing, and the price was dictated by a hard-nosed U.S. government operating with a temporary Congress of only fifty-two members, one man from each state, more than half of them military men. Before a country got the *Kennedy,* that country instituted a very tough program of birth control. Before a nonindustrial country received food, the governments provided heavy penalties for unlicensed births. The freedom to breed was, very definitely, put into cold storage, and when starving millions protested, food shipments were cut off until the starving millions saw the light and obeyed government edicts to use birth control. On the New York Stock Exchange, the stocks of companies in the birth-control field shot out of sight.

Parliamentary democracy was not popular in the United States. The politicians who had sat for centuries in the halls of government without solving even the most pressing problems were sent home to work the fields to help restore American agriculture, for the manna from heaven made an excellent fertilizer. Actually, only a few of the ex-movers and shakers did manual labor, but many fancied themselves to be gentlemen farmers, and it made a good story when it was told to the press by J.J. Barnes, Minister of Supply of the Second Republic.

Admiral Gordon was not totally satisfied with the new government in Washington, but it was better than anything the country had known since the last of the hard-nosed American Presidents, Harry Truman, died in the middle of the twentieth century. Dom began to have hope, as he talked to traditionalists in the services, that a total military dictatorship would be avoided, and that a measure of freedom would be maintained, to be expanded upon in the future. Never, however, would something so precious as a vote be extended to people steeped in ignorance and indolence. The right to vote would be available to all, but it would be earned, and not by owning money or property. The vote could be exercised only by those who, by written test, demonstrated a working knowledge of the choices of free men. The franchise would be available to any person if it was earned, but it was not a God-given right. Future elections would not be won by the man who looked best on television, or by a man who got votes because his father and the voter's father had been Publicrat all their lives.

Admiral Neil Walters took the *Kennedy* on her third trip to Jupiter after completing flight tests on the second of the huge tankers. Admiral Gordon raced him there on the *New Republic,* the *Kennedy's* sister ship. To his pleasure, the old girl beat her younger sister into orbit by two hours and thirty-two minutes.

It was a long trip to Dom, for Doris was Earthside, designing a computer which would link qualified voters to a referendum center in Washington. By the time he got back to the moon, ten million citizens had qualified, and were in a position to let their voices be heard on all questions, not merely who was to sit on the throne of power. An entirely new form of government of the people and by the people was slowly being put into effect.

When she met the shuttle which took him down, she was in full dress uniform. Dom had never seen her look more beautiful. He found her to smell and feel equally wonderful as he seized her in a bear hug and lifted her from her feet. He had only one plan. It involved privacy and Doris. And, in the future, if she didn't go, he didn't go.

"You're not being dignified, admiral," Doris said, tugging at her tunic. "And we're on camera."

Dom looked up into the eye of a television camera. "Again?" he asked.

"This one is special," Doris said. "The media have been released from censorship. We're operating with a free press again, and the network wants to do a full documentary on the first flight of the *Kennedy*."

"Later," Dom said, seizing her arm and trying to lead her away.

"There are orders from on high to cooperate," Doris said.

"J.J.?" Dom asked. She nodded. "Oh, hell," he said. "Let him be interviewed. I'm taking you home."

But he was blocked by another camera crew and a young woman. "Admiral Gordon, we won't take much of your time."

"All right," Dom said. "Let's get on with it."

"We'd like to do one segment of filming on the construction site," the young lady said. A third tanker was taking shape out on the moon. "We can do that after you've had a chance to rest from your trip."

"You're all heart," Dom said.

John Marrow was to conduct the interview with Dom. He cornered Dom. "I think you'd like to know

what goes before," he said. "It'll only take a minute."
He placed Dom in front of a portable monitor.

The introduction to the documentary opened with dramatic closeup shots of Jupiter. The *Kennedy* was superimposed against the gas giant. Marrow's voice was talking about the state of the world at the time of the *Kennedy's* first voyage and of the brave men and women who set out aboard an untested vessel on a mission which would change the world.

"Here's where we come in," Marrow said. "We're on." He faced the camera. "And now a third tanker of the Kennedy class is nearing completion. As she takes shape, out beyond the moon, we have with us the man who designed the original *Kennedy,* a man who has just returned from his third expedition to Jupiter. His friends call him Flash Gordon."

"You're not my friend," Dom said. "To you it's Admiral Gordon."

"Cut," Marrow said. "I'm sorry, admiral. Shall we try again?" He went through his introduction. "And now, Admiral Gordon, can you tell us the results of your latest trip to Jupiter?"

"We brought home the bacon, same as before,"Dom said.

"An apt phrase, admiral, for in a sense that's exactly what you did, isn't it?"

"That's what I said."

"For, indeed, the hold of the *New Republic* contains enough material to furnish food for millions of people."

"To be specific," Dom said, "the hold contains several hundred thousand tons of carbonigenous cloud from the three-thousand-atmosphere layer of the planet Jupiter."

"Now, Admiral Gordon, let's go back to the beginning, when you and J.J. Barnes were designing the original *Kennedy.*"

"J.J. had nothing to do with designing the ship," Dom said. "He was project head. The design was done by me and my team, which included Larry and Doris Gomulka—"

"Cut," Marrow said. "Let's go back to 'let's go back to the beginning.' Roll 'em. Let's go back to the beginning, admiral, to the time when you and your team were designing the original *Kennedy*. I understand that you did not know the true function of the ship. Is that true?"

"We were told that there was an alien ship inside the atmosphere of Jupiter," Dom said.

"Is it true that only one or two men knew the true purpose of the first expedition?"

"I don't know how many," Dom said. "J.J. Barnes knew."

"But you, admiral, soon saw, once you were down in the atmosphere, that J.J. Barnes was a man of true vision, a man with brilliant insight and wisdom?"

"I thought he was crazy," Dom said.

"You no longer feel that way, I'm sure." Marrow laughed.

"I still think he's a nut, but an inspired and very lucky nut. He took a gamble and it paid off. It was a brilliant gamble and we owe a lot to J.J."

"Would you cast your vote for J.J. Barnes as President of the United States?"

"No," Dom said.

"Cut," Marrow said.

"What the fuck kind of a question is that?" Dom demanded.

"Don't you know that J.J. filed for the Presidency in the next election?" Marrow asked.

"No."

"Would you vote for him?"

"No."

"We'll leave that out," Marrow said. "Roll 'em."

He thought for a minute. "Are you a qualified voter, Admiral Gordon?"

"Not yet. I'll probably have to have my wife coach me to pass the test."

Marrow was forming another question when Dom interrupted. "Did J.J. line this up so that I would give him a testimonial as a candidate?"

"Let 'em roll," Marrow said. "We'll cut it out later." He changed tactics. "As the man who designed the *Kennedy* and was her captain on her first voyage, could you, Admiral Gordon, give us your explanation of what some people call a miracle?"

"Well, it wasn't really a miracle," Dom said. "It came at the right time, and that made it seem miraculous. The materials were there. We merely had the hardware to go get them and put them to use. The most puzzling part of it, to most people, is actually the simplest. That part of the miracle is repeated over and over, every day, somewhere on Earth. When the air is overcharged with vapor, the vapor condenses and falls as precipitation. If you overcharge an atmosphere with the proper amounts and the proper compounds of carbon and hydrogen, then the precipation will be in the form of carbon-hydrogen compounds, or carbohydrates."

"Or manna from heaven," Marrow said.

"The ancient Jews called it that," Dom said. "The Talmud said bread rained from heaven. In Icelandic legend, people ate the morning dew; Buddhists called it heavenly oil, perfume, and ointment. It came in a time of troubles, and was called a miracle, just as it comes to us in a time of trouble. The only difference is that instead of a god or goddess bringing it to us, we went out and got it."

"Yes, thanks to the foresight of that great man, J.J.

Barnes," Marrow said, smiling directly into the camera.

"Thanks to Immanuel Velikovsky," Dom said. "Who is long dead."

"Ah, yes," Marrow said.

"That's why the third ship is to be named the *Velikovsky*," Dom said.

Much later, Dom lay in a hammock watching the sun set over the Gulf of Mexico. It was a lovely evening. He felt good. The warm softness of a summer evening caressed his skin. An empty drink glass was in his hand, and he was trying to work up enough energy to go inside and fill it when Doris came out.

"Hey, admiral," she called. "Your interview is on."

He ambled in. He saw himself standing beside John Marrow. He grunted and went to mix a drink, but he was human so he came back to see himself as others saw him. However, he couldn't keep his eyes on his own face, because Doris was standing behind him, looking quite nice.

"You look good in living color," he said.

"You look sleepy."

"I was."

"There are nuts and there are nuts," Dom was saying. "Velikovsky was a nut who lived and wrote in the middle part of the twentieth century. Briefly, he evolved a theory, by bringing together information from hundreds of ancient writings—"

"Material which was highly suspect," Marrow put in.

"Suspect only because of the limitations of early writing," Dom said. "Take the Bible, for example. It was written in Hebrew. Hebrew is a primitive and very inexact language. In Hebrew, as in most ancient languages, one word can mean several things. Thus, depending on the translator, you can read just about anything you want to read into the Bible or any other writings from the early times. Shortly after Velikov-sky's time, for example, a German used the same sources to prove to a lot of people that Earth had been visited by spacers from another planet. You pays your money and you takes your choice. Velikovsky had a slight advantage with thinking people, because he proved to be right in a couple of predictions. He predicted the higher-than-estimated surface tempera-ture on Venus."

"Doesn't that higher surface temperature on Venus play a vital part in Velikovsky's theory?"

"Velikovsky said that Venus was thrown out of the planet Jupiter into an erratic orbit which brought her into near collision with both Mars and the Earth," Dom said.

"At the time of the Exodus, and again in the time of Joshua, in the Bible," Marrow said.

"But the Velikovsky theory didn't account for all known phenomena," Dom said, "so it was treated as a rather scary and very harebrained idea. It was largely forgotten."

"But not by J.J. Barnes," Marrow said.

"Yes," Dom said, "Velikovsky's theory was that the carbonigenous clouds torn out of Jupiter by the planet Venus made carbohydrates fall onto Earth during the moments of near collision. One nut remembered an-other nut and we went off to Jupiter and found it to be, truly, a land of milk and honey."

"At this moment," Marrow said, "a cargo of car-bonigenous cloud from Jupiter is being pumped into a vast cloud chamber on the moon. There, the carbohy-drates will precipitate out, be shaped into loaves, loaves which you and I will be eating in the near fu-ture."

"Well," Dom said, "that's that." He switched off the set.

"He's an insufferable little man," Doris said.

"I don't want to talk about him," Dom said.

"Would you like to review a little history to get ready for the voter's test?"

"Not now."

"Something is on your mind," she said.

"You," he said. "Velikovsky."

"I understand the first," she said, with a leer.

"Was Velikovsky right?"

"At least about the properties of the Jovian atmosphere."

"Was it a lucky guess?"

"He doesn't explain everything, of course," she said. "You're thinking about those frozen mammoths, aren't you?"

"He's the only one who even had a good guess about them."

"Perhaps it's good that everything can't be explained," Doris said. "It leaves us something to worry about and something to learn, a little bit at a time, so that we won't sit around and think about what you're thinking about all the time."

He grinned. "I'll get around to that." He stood and looked out a window. "Mars was a living planet once. The sun may have been hotter, the planet was certainly wetter. A change in orbit would explain why she died, and Velikovsky said Mars had troubles with Venus before she settled down into a stable orbit. Velikovsky uses the changes in Earth calendars to make some good points. People who had good math seemed to make silly mistakes about the length of the day and changed their calendars later. And why, in all of the primitive races, was there a fear of comets?"

"Are you leading up to something?" she asked.

"Envision the orbits of Pluto and Neptune."

"Yes, I see what you mean," she said. "Pluto actually comes inside the orbit of Neptune at one point."

"Will there ever be a collision? Pluto's a small planet. If he got knocked off his orbit and came cruising across the orbits of the inner planets, what would happen?"

"They're not in the same plane, Pluto and Neptune, but I think you have my attention. I'll do some calculations. And that takes care of Velikovsky for the moment. What about taking care of me?"

"I want to do some research," he said. "Can you get me all the observations of the outer planets? Figure a cost on taking one of the new hydropower scouts out there at the next conjunction. I think it's within the next three years."

"You've been thinking about this for some time," she said.

"Do you think the two of us can handle one of the new Explorer class scouts?"

"A second honeymoon to Pluto," she said. "I'm underwhelmed. Don't you have any immediate work I could, ah, help you with?"

She stood and looked into his eyes. She was dressed in shorts and halter. The very feminine spread of her hips reminded him that he did have immediate plans for her.

Pluto would have to wait.

ZACH HUGHES is the pen name of Hugh Zachary, who, with his wife Elizabeth, runs a book factory in North Carolina. Hugh quit a timeclock job in 1963 and turned to writing full-time. He is the author of a number of well-received science fiction novels, and together with Elizabeth, he has turned out many fine historical romances, as well as books in half a dozen other fields.

Hugh Zachary has worked in radio and tv broadcasting and as a newspaper feature writer. He has also been a carpenter, run a charter fishing boat, done commercial fishing, and served as a mate on an anchor-handling tugboat in the North Sea oil fields.

Hugh's science fiction novel, KILLBIRD, is available in a Signet edition.